T0023295

Juventud

"A harrowing international coming-of-age story . . . [*Juventud*] kept me up at night, and that's the highest praise."

—PATRICIA HENLEY, National Book Award Nominated author of *Hummingbird House* and *In the River Sweet*

"Part love story and part mystery novel, *Juventud* is also a tale of the complexities of family, the strains on the ties that bind, and the expectations we place on each other that no one can adequately meet."

—*NEWCITY*

"Blakeslee's striking first novel captures the essence of bring a teenager in late 1990s Colombia. [. . .] This tale of self-discovery and intense first love is spiced with bursts of action and curious twists."

—*PUBLISHERS WEEKLY*

"Among the many things to admire about Vanessa Blakeslee's first novel, *Juventud*, foremost must be its ambition . . . maintaining control over a terrain that, vast as it is, feels nonetheless suited to [Blakeslee's] talent."

—*RAIN TAXI*

"Blakeslee is keenly aware of social injustice and exploitation . . . [*Juventud*] is fiercely cosmopolitan, and at times, feels like equal parts travelogue, political thriller, and bildungsroman."

—NICK RUPERT, *New Orleans Review*

"[*Juventud*] echoes the conflicts of our twenty-first century's transnational, uneasy global culture."

—XU XI, author of *Habit of a Foreign Sky*

Train Shots

"Evidently, Vanessa Blakeslee was somebody's big secret until now. I just don't know how they kept her from us or why they would . . . [*Train Shots*] is a haunting story collection of the first order."

—JOHN DUFRESNE, author of *No Regrets, Coyote*

"*Train Shots* announces an outstanding new voice. Vanessa Blakeslee's stories traverse a trilling range of landscapes and voices, but no matter where her characters find themselves, their struggles with lost love and loneliness are authentic and engrossing and will not soon be forgotten."

—LAURA VAN DEN BERG, author of *The Isle of Youth* and *What the World Will Look Like When All the Water Leaves Us*

PERFECT
CONDITIONS

VANESSA BLAKESLEE

stories

CURBSIDE SPLENDOR PUBLISHING

Published by Curbside Splendor Publishing, Inc., Chicago, Illinois in 2018.

First Edition
Copyright © 2018 by Vanessa Blakeslee

ISBN 978-1-940430-99-7
Designed by Alban Fischer

Manufactured in the United States of America.

www.curbsidesplendor.com

Stories in this collection first appeared in the following publications: "Traps" at *Bridge Eight Literary Magazine*; "Stand by to Disembark" in *Moon City Review* and subsequently in *Joyland*; "Jesus Surfs" in *The Wordstock Ten: Finalists from the 2009 Wordstock Short Fiction Competition* and subsequently in *Atticus Review*; "The Perfect Pantry" by Burrow Press at *Fantastic Floridas*; "Perfect Conditions" in *Grist*; "Sustainable Practices" at *The Good Men Project*; "Clinica Tikal" at *Ascent*; and "Arthur and George: The Voyage Begins" (published originally as "Arthur and George: The Quest") at *Drunken Boat*.

CONTENTS

PERFECT CONDITIONS

TRAPS

Every day on the mountain I awaken to fish or forage, and every day at 4 pm my walkie-talkie crackles with Uncle Mack's voice ordering us down to target practice. Afternoons, I wander to the scrubby clearing beneath his house and help to reposition the bodies made of straw, old t-shirts, and duct tape—effigies of my cousin Melanie, her brother, my aunt. Mack paces behind us in shorts and colorful selections from his iconic t-shirt collection. Today's shirt is stiff and bright black, likely never worn; the front commemorates a visit by the Dalai Lama to Penn State a decade ago. On the back, in slanted white letters, the shirt proclaims, "'Never Give Up!'—His Holiness the Dalai Lama," with a big airbrushed portrait of the Dalai Lama, grinning. Something about the shirt hints at an amateur design—an unofficial vendor hawking wares outside the arena. The shirt may yet end up on one of the dummies. Three weeks ago he retired the baby blue one with the drawing of pedestrians staring into their cell phones, an orderly queue of them walking right off a cliff.

"Aren't Buddhists pacifist vegetarians?" I ask, loading a rifle.

"You want to eat meat this winter?" Uncle Mack squints at me, hands on his trim waist. "Because freeze-dried food makes it really hard to shit. Fire that gun."

I fire. The straw shimmies. "A deer, okay," I say. "Maybe."

"Deer, turkeys, rabbits, you name it." He strolls away, toward the empty crates next to me, my cousin Melanie's usual spot. Nobody else is here yet, but he sets out fresh ammo.

"Why aren't we killing them now, then?" I ask. "Even though I don't want to." I line up my shot. When we talked about straw men back in college, I never pictured this. Only a few years ago, but might as well have been a century.

"If we start killing everything in midsummer, before the animals mature and breed, what protein will we have for winter?"

My shot strikes the shoulder. I stand up to reload, and look around. From the middle of the garden, Melanie waves. She is dragging a sprinkler which is plugged into my uncle's solar unit. My cousin is a better shot than me. All those years I boycotted Thanksgiving because of politics and religion, while she practiced her riflery and hatchet toss. Uncle Mack steps over, adjusts my shoulders. "Whenever you pull a gun, you mean business. Shoot to kill is the rule, not the exception."

"I'd rather shoot someone's foot to scare him off."

"So he can reach into his pocket and blow you away." He points to where the drive dips below the tree line. I know what's coming, but the repetition doesn't seem to faze him. "You see there? That's where they'll come—mobs of them from the cities. They'll roam for as long as they can find gas, and then they'll walk. They'll want our food. They'll think we're selfish because we saw the signs and prepared. You know what parents will do for starving kids?"

I stir a finger in the box of bullets. "Maybe we shouldn't be selfish. Maybe we should give them some food, and you know," I nod toward the imaginary hordes in the driveway, "suggest they move along."

"My property, my way," Uncle Mack says. He rubs his nose, laughs. "You don't like it, you can leave."

We move on to crossbows. I'm better with that—the heft and release of the bow feels more natural. Still haven't killed anything with one, though. I worry about my usefulness as an orphan relation; within days of our bugging in at my uncle's compound two months ago, a hierarchy quickly and quietly formed. None of what I studied of psychology in college mattered; I received crash courses in what went to the compost pile and what went to the goats, how to live with less electricity, how to dry and can what we gathered. The nuke that went off in the city had been a strategic one, the fallout here minimal; that alone has my uncle convinced the Deep State pulled a false flag.

"They need a war, a last grab for cheap energy," he says at dinner. "The Arctic's in serious meltdown, and a few nukes are all we've got to stall a massive methane burp. Either that or we need a volcano to erupt."

I aim my bow and fill the straw man with arrows.

*

The next morning, behind the house, I fill the water trough for the goats while Uncle Mack climbs across the roof. He stops now and then to adjust a solar panel. A stone's throw away, something rustles an evergreen bush—a rabbit sits up on his haunches, turns and scampers off. I'm still constipated from last night's freeze-dried beef stroganoff. So much for my five solid years as a disciplined pescatarian. Even if I had a rifle with me I would have to be very quick, not to mention a great shot.

"Uncle Mack," I call. "I want to learn how to set traps. Would you be able to show me?"

"You gotta set a lot of them, check them all the time."

"Do I have anything else better to do?"

He swears at the solar panel he's holding, stomps around up there. Cold water drenches my calves; the trough runs over. "You going to skin and butcher the game when you bring it back?" he yells, finally. "Pull out the guts? 'Cause that's what you have to do."

The billy goat comes up and rubs his head against my waist, his odor filling my nose and mouth. The goats stink but I love them anyway. "I'll learn," I say. "Maybe I'll be good at it. Maybe I'll be better with traps than guns."

Indoors is cool, no A/C, from the house being built against the rock. On the far side of the living room, where someone else would keep a widescreen TV, books line the shelves floor to ceiling. Many are hardcover, gold-embossed classics, but the DVD cabinet contains worn softcovers: homesteading and survival manuals. He pulls out *The Trapper's Bible, Basic Butchering of Livestock and Game, How to Survive in the Woods*, and a few others.

"For your stack," he says, meaning the field and foraging guides he handed me weeks ago, to reinforce what he'd shown me in the woods.

The trees are still but the woods are not. Insects rasp and beat, birds flutter and chirp. I walk right through a cobweb and shake out my arms, unable to get the sticky feeling off me. Mack, up ahead, steps around the cobwebs, then resumes the path. A strand of blackberry bushes lines a rocky outcropping, most of the berries picked clean by Melanie and me, plus deer and bear, but a few remain. Lots of flat rock slabs around. Here Uncle Mack sets up our first primitive fall-trap. "Easy, huh?" he says. "You try."

I find the appropriate sticks and rocks, and set up the trap. Only the rock drops, the stick snaps; my heart jolts. I get a new stick, reset the trap, and the rock falls again—scrapes my knuckles this time. "I don't know if I can do this," I say. "I need more than just to survive. I need joy, I need beauty."

"You're not enjoying this?" In the shade, Uncle Mack has set up two traps outside animal holes. "Puts me in a zone, once I get going."

"But what's the point? To just 'keep going'?"

"That's the path of the warrior: to keep going, come out on the other side—whatever that is." He strolls over, shuffles through his handful of sticks, resets my trap. "Don't think so much."

We follow a game trail up, then down, then up, setting ground snares with a spool of fishing line. "Easy, huh?" he says. Finished, he starts back but I tell him I'm going to hike farther up the ridge. The sky is a weird bright haze, the air moist and hot. A turtle shies at the edge of the trail; I pause, then hike past him. Only after I scramble over some boulders at the top do I wonder: should I have looked at him as food, or did I read something about turtle meat and parasites? I sit cross-legged, blood seeping from my scraped knuckle. Here you can see for miles, across the Delaware and the flat of New Jersey. The war will come here. There will be punishing drought. And we are bombing how many countries now? What they don't tell you is you can live without hope. When you let go of that, fear dissolves as well. But then what—do I want to spend my days hunting and trapping? Am I capable of killing, even to defend myself? And then when does the killing end? A burrow remains beneath a nearby tree. I scoot over, set up a fall-trap.

*

That night Uncle Mack hums over a pot of boiling pasta. I rinse tomatoes and shred what I have gathered from the yard—plantain, dandelion, lamb's quarters—into bite-sized chunks. The lettuce turned sour weeks ago. "Weed salad," he says, "just like Mom used to make." He dumps a can of white beans into the sauce. I frown. I don't care if I see pasta or beans for the rest of my life, but I keep this to myself. Truck deliveries have been intermittent; families are hungry.

The two of us sit at one end of the long dining table, the chandelier dim overhead. "You think we'll have luck with those traps we set today?" I ask. I spear some beans and greens together, mix up the taste. "Or you think that was a waste of time?"

"Depends what walks under them," he says. Sauce dribbles down his chin; he mops it up, staring ahead. "Depends if you used bait. Which we didn't." Darkness shrouds the front room of the house, his large telescope immobile, dull with dust. A birdcage sways empty among the feral houseplants. "If we're lucky we'll get a squirrel or a chipmunk."

"Luck doesn't sound too encouraging."

"Just set more traps." He picks out a dandelion stem, points the fluff at me. "Cast a wider net, literally." The dandelion disappears into his mouth. He chews and swallows fast.

Beside me is the messy stack of books we pulled from his library earlier. I pull over *The Trapper's Bible* and leaf through it. "Fish traps, now those are interesting. I'd love to go fishing tomorrow." I eat the rest of my salad, except for the dandelion. The yellow heads pile up at the bottom. "Do you enjoy this, Uncle Mack? Is living like this enough for you?"

"Enjoy?" He frowns. "How do you think we lived before we sold out for trinkets and junk? Set some traps, fished, fucked. Made war on each other with stones and sticks." His nostrils flare. From the hillside behind us comes the faint cry of the youngest goat. "Poisoned and radiated the whole goddamn place."

Silence beats. "I enjoyed myself today," I say quietly. "Thanks."

He rises, gathers the plates. "You want to go fishing, look up some traps. If kids in Bolivia can make them, so can you."

Some of the books still smell unused: sleek field guides, the photos vivid and bright. Some, like *The Trapper's Bible*, are underlined, notes scrawled in the margins from a previous owner. "For possible use on the Six Mile trail?" crawls up the side in neat, antiquated cursive, with an arrow pointing to the trap illustration. The *Foxfire* books contain old stories and anecdotes, along with black-and-white shots of Appalachia—bearded, wiry men and sour-faced women. One man holds up a rattlesnake that matches his height. Other photos depict the steps to build a log cabin, and how to make lye for soap. I find no shortage of traps; the more sophisticated require twine to bend and tie saplings, a hatchet to make notches in wood. All evolved from centuries of trial and error, as organic as the humus of the forest floor, and in the last century, just abandoned. Traps have a sense of fair play aligned with the universe. Be aware and avoid, be unaware and get caught. If caught you might escape, but not

without injury. In the woods and marshes, death feeds life. A truth
so obvious we have forgotten.

*

A week, maybe two, goes by. The days blur. We build and set the
traps where the waterfall meets the creek, but the fish are very small.
We have better luck with the snares: squirrels, rabbits, and once, a
small fawn, delicate and beautiful. He wriggles fiercely and I cut
the line; a second later there is nothing of the creature, nothing but
a crash in the brush and he is gone. The cardinal that lives above
flies to and fro, watching me.

One day we're in the clearing, the shooting range dummies soggy
and losing their straw after a few thunderstorms. Under a tree Uncle
Mack skins a rabbit that was caught in the morning's snare. Blood
and entrails moisten the dirt, the odor metallic and earthy all at
once. Clouds pass overhead; the blades glint. "Do you hear something?" I ask.

A breeze swirls the boughs above the driveway, but the crest
where the gravel disappears from view remains empty. We freeze.
"I hear shuffling," I say. Our relatives who live nearby all have walk-
ie-talkies; no visits happen unannounced.

Uncle Mack drops his knife and grabs his rifle. He puts a finger
to his lips. A bomb struck Hawaii last week; all over the country,
cities are emptying out. I grab my rifle and we creep down the
driveway. Uncle Mack whips his walkie-talkie off his waist, radios
his brother. A gang would have to pass the houses of my relatives
first, all of whom are heavily armed. We would have heard gunshots
from down the hill.

No one answers Uncle Mack. He fires a warning shot; birds
screech and scatter.

"Hold on," I say. "Unless some gang is invading with karate and
knives, I doubt anything's happened."

"You heard of silencers?" He ducks behind a tree. We are

close to where the driveway dips and curves now. He aims, finger on trigger.

A girl staggers up the hill, hair mussed and grimy, the loose remains of French braids. She shoulders a backpack, pauses to bend over and catch her breath. It's my sister. No one's heard from her since the last election.

"Put that down, Uncle Mack," I say. "It's Cara."

"Hi," she pants, lunging up the remainder of the hill. "You look like you've been killing something."

"I have," I say. "You walked here? From Massachusetts?"

"Sure did." She slings off her backpack, her stale body stench more pungent than the rabbit. She tells us how she remembered what Uncle Mack said a long time ago, about the Appalachian Trail running along the next ridge from our relatives' cluster of properties. "Thanks for not shooting me," she says to him.

"You armed?" He lowers his rifle. Today he wears a faded polo shirt with the logo of a local pizzeria long defunct. "Trail's got to be dangerous right now."

"Actually, no." Cara describes how she traveled mostly with a group of med school students who had caught the trail in Western Massachusetts, same as she did. They'd helped each other out: shared food, carried each other's belongings when someone got too tired, built fires, sang songs. That she couldn't have made the journey alone. They had parted ways near Wind Gap; some had family they wanted to meet up with in New Jersey and farther south. She didn't believe she'd see any of them again.

Our uncle waved toward the house. "Come on up, shower. We'll be firing up the grill soon. Looks like you need some protein."

Cara and I hug. "I wish you'd brought your friends," I say. "I'm sorry."

"Zombie hordes," she says, and laughs into my shoulder. I slip on her backpack and rest my rifle under the tree. An owl gracefully sails over our path and the clearing, a dark form limp in his claws.

STAND BY TO DISEMBARK

The day after a few of the ship's factory workers pulled a joke on him, Crazy Paul flipped out and beat up a table with a gaff. Rumor was that the army had found Paul mentally unstable after too many tours in the Middle East and let him go—how many tours was too many was what Quentin wanted to know, but didn't ask. The running joke about Crazy Paul amongst the crew was that he believed the little rabbit tattoo high on his neck whispered things into his ear.

Dang, their crew leader, sent Paul up on deck for a time out. At lunch break Crazy Paul told them that he'd been wandering around to clear his head when he happened to pause outside the wheelhouse.

"We're not going to off-load in Dutch Harbor," Paul said, rubbing his neck. "I overheard the Captain talking." Everyone within earshot leaned toward Paul, cursing and barraging him with questions. "Will you listen?" Paul said, blinking and stuttering. He clenched his fork, adjusted his hardhat. He'd scrawled U.S. ARMY on the back in slanted block letters, despite his discharge.

"The company's planning to off-load at sea. That means we're going to have to fish another trip before Cascade lets anyone off. Another three months."

"Bullshit," Quentin said. "That's breach of contract."

"How else you gonna get off this ship if they don't? Cascade Fishing gonna fly in a helicopter just for you?" Paul wagged his head, shoveled a bite, kept talking as he chewed. "It's an old trick, I'm telling you. Companies do this all the time."

Jason, Quentin's bunkmate, stared, chopsticks hovering above his noodles. Quentin leaped up, climbed to the wheelhouse, and rapped on the door. Thirty seconds, and finally the captain swung open the door; it bounced against the wheelhouse.

"Jesus."

"I hear you're not letting us off," Quentin said.

"What you gonna do if I don't?"

"There's at least a dozen other guys who have contracts up, same day as mine. You want a lawsuit?"

The captain flung back his head and laughed.

Quentin kept talking. His words slurred, his brain snapping and crackling like aluminum foil in a microwave. Fatigue—this argument sounded nothing more than a drunk's speech. When was the last time he'd had a drink? No idea. Did none of the men who wanted off have the balls to raise hell like he was? Why not? Why was he raising hell? Did Crazy Paul even know what he was talking about? Or was this lack of restraint his own unraveling? He heard himself saying, "You've got to get me off this ship. I won't make this easy for you."

"Don't worry, you've made that clear," the captain said. He slammed and latched the door.

Quentin climbed back down below. The men were scraping their plates, exiting from lunch. "So how'd your little talk go with the Captain?" said Marcel, brushing past too closely, just to annoy him. "Did you run to him, make a big stink?" Quentin fought the urge to pick up a gaff and beat the nearest bench or beam, like Crazy Paul had. "And what if I did?" he said, Marcel's face just inches from his. "Or what, is that crazy? No one ever call the Captain on this bullshit?" Marcel laughed, said, "Nope," and slinked off. Was everyone laughing at him?

Quentin resumed his station and started sorting fish. He and

Jason faced a giant mound from the nets dropped in earlier. A few big halibut, weighing about a hundred pounds each, had wedged like boulders among the catch, mostly atka mackerel. The men threw out the halibut; by law they couldn't take them. Quentin used to try and save as many as he could, sprint up on deck and heave them overboard. "Let Cascade Fishing breach contract," he said. He was chucking fish onto the cutter table so hard that every so often one skidded off. "When I get back, I'll be outside the company office in Seattle first thing, with the meanest lawyer I can find."

"Oh, yeah?" Jason said. He was a couple of years younger than Quentin, a Mormon kid who'd screwed up his mission trip. Someone found out he'd slept with a girl and reported him. He'd signed with Cascade as a sort of spiritual quest, or punishment—Quentin wasn't sure which. "Sounds like your talk with him was pretty useless, man," Jason said. "Why not forget it? What are you so eager to get back to?"

But Quentin wasn't eager to get back.

His mother had begged him not to enlist in the military just to return in pieces like his father, whose war had been the everyday kind, the battle to earn his keep and his family's, too. Instead of the military Quentin signed on for a three-month stint on a deep sea fishing vessel. All he knew was that an overwhelming urge had overtaken him—to busy his hands, to fill his mouth and nose and eyes with the unfamiliar and concrete. On those first few days aboard, gaining his sea legs and popping Dramamine, all he could think about was leaving with his twenty thousand in the bank—the hardest money he'd likely ever earn in his life, money he needed to get on his feet when he got back, like his friend Oakley had bragged about. Then Quentin could pay his mother's rent so they wouldn't lose the house. He hadn't been aboard a week, assigned to a group working the winches and ropes, when a crewman's sleeve got snagged; the crewman shouted and the others struggled to free him, but too late. The mooring mishap cost the unlucky fisherman two fingers. Now, as the metal blade whirred and he worked the cutter, he wondered how his father was doing, if he'd remember Quentin or be too far gone. The day his father had lost his temper in the control tower, rattling his co-workers and jeopardizing dozens of airplanes, had been what forced his early retirement. Twenty-five years in that tower, at what cost?

*

That night, when Jason whispered his prayers, Quentin mouthed a few lines of his own. He wanted to be sure no one heard, even though the ship never slept, but emitted a constant *boom*— silence—*boom*. But, exhausted as he was, he couldn't sleep. The thoughts never stopped. *How could you be such an idiot, to listen to Oakley? What kind of moron signs up for a job that's just as dangerous as a tour in Afghanistan—at least there you might have risked your life with your friends. How naïve could you be? You deserve to lose your fucking mind.* He swung his legs over the bunk and pulled on his clothes.

Above deck, late summer wallowed in its brief night. He lurched for the railing and caught his breath. Frigid out there in the wind, the sun crushed to purple at the horizon. The ship bucked and pitched, its lights cast over the side, but he hung on, inched forward. He ought to be on a safety line. Walls of waves, dark grey, arose like moving hillsides and swiftly disappeared to black. A hypnotic pull, a terrifying abyss. If a man jumped, he'd never be found. The ship rolled upward; he stumbled and retreated, headed back below deck. This time, sleep overcame him.

*

"Stand by to haul back," the ship's loudspeakers droned.

All six in the cabin tugged on their sweats, Grundens suits and wool-lined rubber boots. Then headed down to eat the same breakfast: tasteless scrambled eggs that remained dry clumps no matter how much salt and pepper you used or how long you chewed, the bacon so brittle it scraped your throat, even as you washed it down with coffee. Then a hasty bathroom break before shift, the many layers of clothing bulky and cumbersome. What he wouldn't give for the choice of a meal, or a bottle of tabasco sauce for his eggs, or just fifteen minutes to himself, to do anything he wanted. He wondered if the military was this much of a prison, or how the men around him could give up so much liberty to earn a living. How had he? For all his mother's fussing over the dangers of the turbulent Arctic seas, he could still hear her clearly tell an old friend over the phone how thankful and relieved she was to have a son who had a sense of honor and duty to family during hard times—"And I'm hoping it will be good for him, you know—he'll have an adventure," she had added. Packing his bags, he thought the same thing. Maybe better that he had not weighed the personal cost to himself but convinced himself of the Jack London fantasy, or else he might have wimped out, cancelled the flight.

That morning Quentin told Dang he couldn't work below in the factory anymore, something Dang didn't like to hear from his fastest sorter. When he asked why, Quentin just mumbled, "Please," and something about needing a break.

The sky was blue and cloudless, and the air tingled Quentin's cheeks. His head felt lighter, probably because he was no longer bent over an endless pile of fish. When the nets were hauled back and stored along the ship's sides, the loose fish fell out; trapped between the nets and deck walls, they rotted. Above deck hung gutted fish which the Japanese deckhands had strung up on lines to dry in the salty open air and sunlight—an old practice. The Japanese ripped off chunks of the shredded fish as they hurried underneath. One of them offered Quentin some jerky, and he did his best to respectfully decline. Inhaling fish stench as he jumped nets, ran winches, and wielded his gaff was enough to nearly make him vomit, never mind the sight of the men feasting on those grisly dried strips of fish.

For now, though, the deck saved him from talking in circles with Jason, Crazy Paul, and the rest over the captain's decision to off-load or not. Being quick to anger, repetition, forgetting where he was, paranoia—that was the kind of thing his father had begun to display, his first symptoms. His father had worked as an air traffic controller, a job that suited his meticulous and energetic personality. When Quentin was in tenth grade, his father's behavior changed drastically. First his mother discovered missed payments, slight deviations in an otherwise perfect record of his keeping their finances in top shape. One night, months later, his father insisted he couldn't fall asleep because he heard rats scurrying beneath the bed, made Quentin's mother lift the mattress and tear off the bedding, revealing nothing. His father had been only forty-nine. Now he was in a home.

At shift-break Quentin headed down to the galley with Mike, one of the few others above deck who spoke English. Mike was a recovering crystal meth addict. Quentin had never seen him take a shower or change clothes in the six months they'd been aboard; his presence made Quentin miss the clean company of his friends. They'd all played baseball together on his high school team. The first baseman had won a full scholarship to the state university and would have started classes by now. The catcher had enrolled in a coding boot camp and tried to convince Quentin, who felt too daunted by the prospect of student loan debt and too undecided about a major, to learn how to code, too. But Quentin had shrugged it off; spending hours staring into a glowing screen, trying to focus on learning an intricate new language, didn't appeal, although the prospect of a solid income did. "Maybe when I get back," Quentin had said. Even Oakley was taking classes to become an EMT, thinking about nursing school and maybe joining the Army reserves. Those who were studying or working close to home would be getting together this time of year for weekend games in the park. Would running bases have cleared his head, helped point a path toward what he might claim for himself while still being a good son? If he lost fingers, or worse, he'd never play a game again.

The cold made detecting all but the most putrid smells difficult—most of the time Quentin was thankful for that. Still, he cringed at the layers of grime and fish scales decorating Mike's arms, the fuzzy brown of his rotting teeth. He was like something they might dredge up in the nets—a barnacled, malformed half-man, half-creature of the deep. "Did anybody come up and ask if you wanted to get off yet?" Quentin asked him.

"Nope," Mike said. He frowned and scratched his elbow. "But there's supposed to be a list. You gotta sign your name if you wanna get off."

In the galley, seven factory workers claimed they'd signed, but no one recalled who was going around collecting names. Quentin choked down his skirt steak and potatoes, furious. Was this a joke? Why couldn't he get a straight answer—was he deliberately being lied to? He felt like the whole goddamn boat was playing a trick on him.

Before second shift he stormed up to Sasaki, the crew leader on deck. But Sasaki started shaking his head before Quentin had finished shouting at him. "No list," Sasaki said, arms folded. "We unload at sea. You stay."

"Sorry, not staying," Quentin answered. "If there's a list, my name better be on it. I'm getting off this ship when my contract's through."

Sasaki jabbed his finger into Quentin's chest, then his own. "Good workers stay."

His father had been a good air traffic controller, Quentin thought. Exceptional, his coworkers had said. Quentin's family had thrown the retirement party, rented out a reception hall. His father's condition was genetic, and the mental gymnastics of tracking planes in the air had possibly staved off the onset for some time. Quentin had factored this in when he'd signed the dotted line with Cascade. He was young and fit; what did he have to worry about? The doctors mentioned a test he could take to find out if he was a carrier. Not until he'd spent a few weeks in the factory with Crazy Paul's PTSD and the stories of crewmen lost overboard in rough seas, the gruesome tales of electrical fires and explosions, severe burns and gouged eyes, did he swallow his gullibility and wished he hadn't declined. These men were scarred, pushed to the brink for so long some of them had forgotten anything different—as if Cascade had fed them through the cutter. And yet so many signed on, year after year, for the lump paycheck. He told Mike to flag him down if he spotted the officer with the list, that he and the others didn't deserve to be played around with.

"Relax," Mike said, adjusting his cap. "Cascade loves to pull this shit. It's not like they won't let you off. Eventually."

The loudspeaker crackled to life: "Stand by to haul back."

More nets were coming in.

Where was the first mate? He should have a clipboard, be taking names. No one around but the crew. Lately he had caught himself forgetting what he was doing, and he'd stand there momentarily confused, exhausted. The doctors had claimed Quentin had a fifty-percent chance of being a carrier; if he did, his chances of his mind eroding by mid-life was one-hundred percent. Terror would set in as he fought to stay alert around the cutter while the ship pitched and rolled. If he ended up losing a hand or puncturing an artery, what then? He might as well have gone to Afghanistan. He couldn't recall ever seeing an officer with a list go around and take names of those who didn't want to renew their contracts; the very conversations of the previous forty-eight hours blurred into mirage. Was it possible he was dreaming up this list, that his mind was so far gone? Or maybe the officer had come around but, dazed by fatigue, Quentin had missed him.

"Stand by to haul back," the loudspeaker boomed again.

The enormous nets dragged up from the sea, stretched with squirming catch. The night before he'd dreamed a similar scene:

He was stomping around in ten inches of freezing saltwater, the fish piled up high as the decks. His frosty breath spewed clouds as he sorted and tossed the catch. Jason called him over, showed him a silver salmon, eerie among the green-black mackerel. "I don't know what he's doing this far out," Jason said. "Must have gotten lost in a current." Then Jason chucked the salmon to Crazy Paul, who sliced off its head at the cutter. The silver salmon, headless, slid onto the packing table where the Vietnamese with cigarettes hanging from their mouths packed the fish into the metal freezer trays.

"Stand by to haul back."

If he didn't get off, the days ahead promised more sorting, packing, and then freezer break, when they heaved out the trays of packed fish from the hydraulic freezers and hauled the frozen blocks to store at the bottom of the ship. Usually the ship would be rolling, the blocks slamming into the men's chests as they caught them.

He and Jason had been assigned freezer break after Jason had just come aboard. They became friends fast—Jason had yanked him aside when one of those fifty-pound blocks of fish flew out of an unlatched freezer and might have killed Quentin right there. They were getting no rest, and Jason soon developed a raging fever. Quentin didn't think the kid would last a week.

Now, the only other sounds were the mechanical groans of the ship, the sea and wind, bursts of Japanese. Quentin clung to a mast and closed his eyes. The list had to exist, as sure as those black walls of icy water—now churning and white-capped as far as the eye could see.

*

The nets pulled in and dropped, and something was wrong. The Japanese waved their arms and shouted to one another. Among the enormous stack of flapping mackerel were tusks, ribs, and skulls. A few of the Japanese crew scavenged for smaller bones to hide in their boot flaps and underneath their Grundens. Some held up skulls and passed tusks back and forth. Sasaki shooed his men away from the catch, but they ignored him.

Word spread quickly. Soon everyone from the factory emerged from below and surrounded the odd treasures. Quentin crowded next to Crazy Paul and Jason. Mike dug through the pile with the Japanese.

"What is this?" Quentin asked Crazy Paul.

"The Walrus Graveyard," he explained. "They swim here to die. They know by instinct."

"And them?" Jason asked, pointing to the fishermen looting the bone pile. "They seem pretty excited."

"Tusks are worth a lot in Asia. They get ground into potions, sold as medicine."

Quentin wondered if this was another daytime hallucination like his dream about the silver salmon. Or another Arctic mirage, like the land he thought he'd seen the other day, which had prompted his stroll above deck the night before, when he couldn't sleep. Just a trick of the horizon after too many hours of sunlight.

Mike held up a tusk longer than his arm, weighed the trophy before him, and, apparently satisfied, picked his way out of the wriggling catch. "Better hurry up if you want anything," he said. "Captain's on his way, and we're supposed to dump all of it back." He shouldered the tusk, headed below.

"You want anything?" Quentin asked Jason.

"Nah," he replied. "But, hey, someone came around the factory asking who wanted to get off."

"Who? Where'd he go?"

"Some officer handed out the list, said to pass it around below. I didn't sign it, so I don't know."

So there was a list. Then why had he struggled so much in getting a straight answer? Would the officers have sent a list around if he hadn't stormed up to the wheelhouse and confronted the Captain in the first place—when none of the others would? Quentin picked up a piece of skull and hurled it overboard, the bone sucked under the swirling, washing machine madness.

*

Quentin asked Dang if he could return to the factory, and Dang agreed but switched him out with Crazy Paul, who was working cutter. Paul hated arbitrary authority and resented taking orders from the Vietnamese in particular—shrimp fishermen with more warm-water experience than here in the Arctic —despite Dang being the most mild-mannered supervisor aboard. In Vietnam, Dang had been an accountant, but his degree didn't count for much in the U.S. Quentin liked talking to Dang, who was about the same age as his father.

"You know who has the paper, for the men to sign who want to get off?" Quentin asked Dang.

The crinkle-eyed man shrugged, dwarfed by his oversized suit. "You ask a lot of questions today," he said, peering up at Quentin. Dang grinned. "Work first, questions later."

Jason smirked, chucking the good fish onto the table where Quentin now commanded the cutter, slicing off heads. Crazy Paul kept his back to them as he sorted fish. Jason held up two rubber-gloved fingers at Quentin, making hopping motions with them.

Quentin flipped Jason the bird for finding his situation so funny—getting paired with someone widely deemed the voyage idiot. How long until his only friend would realize that he might be coming unhinged like Crazy Paul, and make fun of him? Just how crazy was Paul, after all those missions outside Kabul? Could strenuous conditions trigger a dormant gene to kick in early, impossible to reverse, if it hadn't already? When he got off the ship, was he going to live any differently, and how?

Quentin decided to test Paul. He fed the cutter slowly, and the sorted fish backed up on the other end. Paul eyed them piling up; Quentin had thrown off his rhythm. Paul muttered to himself as he hurled the fish toward the cutter, unaware of how Quentin was throwing him off. Quentin laughed, the first reprieve he'd felt in days. If only he could laugh more, he might cling to sanity.

But Paul stepped back and let out a roar of frustration. He seized a gaff, began banging away at a post. Jason and Yasek, the biggest workers on board, were laughing so hard that their breath billowed out white and quickly around them.

Dang swung over to their cutter, gestured to Paul. Through the holes in his knit face mask, Dang's eyes narrowed. He raised his chin, asked sharply, "What's going on?"

Jason nodded toward Paul and made the rabbit ears sign, still grinning. Dang pulled Paul to the side and told him to take a break. Then Dang dragged Marcel over from the packing table so they wouldn't fall behind, and Quentin's laugh quickly died. He exchanged a look with Jason, who frowned. When Marcel grabbed a fish wrong, the fin stabbed him through his rubber glove.

"How long you been on this ship?" Quentin asked him. "Seven months? When are you going to stop pretending you don't know what you're doing?"

Marcel glared but said nothing. He sorted only more slowly now, rubbing his hand through the pierced glove. He had once told Quentin he wanted to be an actor when he finished with Cascade, get on a reality TV show—maybe part of the reason he drummed up drama, although Quentin could care less. He should leave the cutter, go back to sorting. Their bag wage depended on how many fish they processed, and if he was going to lose his mind or a limb working a commercial fishing vessel he was sure as hell going to make the most money he could. And he sure wasn't going to lose fingers because of Marcel.

"Come on, quit slowing us down," Quentin said to Marcel. "Get to work."

"You can't order me around," Marcel replied. A smug smile broke over his face, and he puffed out his chest. "I've got the list."

Quentin flicked the switch; his cutter ground to a halt. The ship swooped up and down in the charging seas, and he waited a moment. Then he used gravity to his advantage and lunged at Marcel, who staggered back, then swatted a fish in his face. Stunned, Quentin grappled for Marcel but his hands slid because of the wet gloves. "You hit me with a fish again, I'll kill you," Quentin shouted. "Now give me the goddamn list."

The ship pitched again. Now Marcel was on top, breath stinging his face. Both stumbled backward, Dang marching toward them, yelling.

Yasek and Jason broke them up. Yasek pressed to Quentin's ear. In his Polish accent and in between excited breaths, he said, "I know you are thinking of home. Settle down."

Quentin gulped air, nodded. Dang roared at them—never were they to abuse the catch for such a stupid disagreement. Quentin seized his chance. "Give me the list," he told Marcel. "Now."

Dang gave a sharp nod. Marcel whimpered, fumbled underneath his gear, and produced plastic-sheathed packet. Quentin held the pen in his freezing fist and scribbled his signature in big letters that looped over the names above. Without a word, Marcel returned the paper and pen to the plastic baggie, replaced it under his suit, then slithered back to the packing table. Quentin picked his way through the fish, back to the cutter; Crazy Paul slipped back to his place and resumed sorting. Quentin kept his head down. One-eyed fish heads piled up at the cutter. At shift's end he gave Paul a thump on the back, said he only intended to joke, although he didn't admit it to Jason or the others.

*

The next morning, word passed through the galley that the vessel would off-load at Dutch Harbor after all, and remain in shipyard for two weeks. Those who didn't want to sign a three-month extension could leave. Quentin's jaw slackened with relief. Soon he'd be on the couch, watching the World Series. If he wanted to he could take a nap during the game. He'd be able to sleep through the night: eight, nine, ten hours if he wanted. He could even invite a girl over.

In the shower, he wept.

The Aleutians made a beautiful sight on either side as they sailed up to the mainland, even though the islands appeared little more than treeless green rocks. They could see for miles. The masts and hulls of Dutch Harbor dotted the distance.

Those whose contracts were finished ate, showered, and stood by to disembark. In the cabin, Quentin donated his sweats and gear to the men who were staying. He handed Jason his rubber gloves and gaff.

Marcel stuck his head in the doorway. "So when you coming back?" he sneered.

"There're a million ways to make money besides doing this," Quentin said, zipping his duffel bag. "Good luck."

He welcomed the odd hug of his street clothes as he bounded up the stairwell, the tautness of crisp jeans and a button-down flannel shirt. Hair whipping against his cheek, he waved goodbye to Sasaki and shook Dang's hand. Most of those men would stay on that ship for years; he hoped that didn't happen to Jason. He was the last one Quentin bid goodbye to.

"Don't dream of fish," Quentin said, squeezing his friend's shoulder.

"Only women," Jason replied, grinning.

The gangway moaned and shimmied under the men's weight. Midway across, Quentin realized Jason was calling after him. He teetered there, the last one off, duffel cramping his shoulder and the loom of the ship jarring, suddenly unsure which direction felt like his life—the days spent onboard or the unfathomable ones ahead. He'd all but forgotten how it felt to sit in the backyard, sun warming his face and neck, and sip a glass of iced tea. Maybe he'd spend some time in his father's woodworking shed. Maybe he'd work some odd jobs for a while, not enroll in courses. Take a slower, more mindful approach; with twenty grand in the bank, why not? He wondered if, during his time at sea, he'd passed the point of no return. If when he got back, he would take the genetic test, or prefer not to know. If his father would still recognize him. As soon as he asked the question, he was certain of the answer.

At the deck rail, Jason waved his arms wildly. The sweatshirt Quentin had given him just fit his broad frame. Jason cupped his hands around his mouth and shouted down: "I said, stay out of prison, when you get back."

"What?" Quentin yelled, squinting.

"I mean"—Jason's voice echoed off the hull—"don't live in your head so much, or in front of a screen. Keep your spirit."

Quentin's sole left the gangway metal, the sun casting his shadow before him—slanted and gigantic, longer than life. Onshore, beneath the sandy grit, the ground pressed back even and solid. He walked on at a clip, shadow a steady bob, always a few steps ahead.

JESUS SURFS

The sunlight glared off Eduardo's shades as he headed toward the beach on his four-wheeler. Usually he didn't kick up such big puffs of dust on the road, even when the surf report lured him out of bed before dawn; today he wore his bandana like a mask over his nose and mouth so that he wouldn't choke. The rumor at the bars in Santa Teresa the night before was that some badass surfer had appeared out of nowhere, and nobody knew where he came from or even his name. This was certainly nothing new, and Eduardo had pushed back his chair, ready to call it a night, when someone told the story of the near-drowning in Mal Pais that morning. Few but the best locals were even able to paddle out to catch the breaks. A gringo on a rented board had been pulled out of the soup by the stranger. Because of the rough conditions, hardly anyone witnessed what happened next. But those who dropped their boards and rushed over to where the limp gringo lay on the sand swore that the surfer who carried him to shore leaned over, cupped his hands over the gringo's mouth and sucked in a giant, slow, rasping breath. Then the surfer turned and spewed a bucket's worth of salt water back into the surf.

Now, underneath the coco palms on the same stretch of beach in Mal Pais, Eduardo rolled up and powered off the four-wheeler. A bevy of identical sand-splattered ATVs rested there. The morning surf, just as the daily report predicted, was ripping clean and well overhead.

But he spotted none of his friends out on the water; the dozen or so locals with boards hung back near the trees, heads bent together in conversation. Some of them studied the surf in silence. Board tucked beneath his arm, Eduardo approached his group of friends.

"Somebody poison the water overnight?" he called. But no one cracked a smile.

"None of us can get out," said Don, his arms folded in front of his t-shirt, a faded relic from Half Moon Bay.

"Except him." Don pointed to the figure shredding the big break farthest from the beach.

Eduardo laughed. "That's impossible," he said. Conditions were smooth as glass and better than they'd seen all week.

"The stranger's good, mai, you'd have to be blind to not see that after two minutes watching the guy," Don said. But Eduardo wasn't convinced. He tied his leash to his ankle and charged for the water.

He threw himself onto his board and paddled toward the rising waves. After a minute he looked back and saw that he hadn't moved more than six feet. He jumped off his board into the knee-deep water, but the undertow, usually like quicksand underneath his feet, didn't exist. The Pacific was as gentle as a lake.

He tried again to get out. Waves splashed in his face, and he was even able to reach deeper water and duck-dive under a large wave speeding toward him, but the force of the wave underneath pushed him far back. His friends were right: even though he was paddling hard and the board seemed to be gliding along, he was stuck on shore as if he was paddling against an invisible wall.

At last, out of breath and sputtering salt water and frustration, he surrendered and trudged back up the beach.

He expected his friends to laugh as he had at them, but they just regarded him in silence. He joined them in the beating sun, and they watched the stranger dropping down the faces of waves that were like huge, rolling hillsides. Eduardo watched until his eyes hurt and his skin was hot and dry.

Who was this stranger? The locals wanted to know. He'd been out there since dawn; when was he going to come in? Two dogs trotted on the beach, chasing blue land crabs back into holes, and every so often the dogs paused, their ears and tails lifted, to gaze at the waves. When the stranger finally paddled in, the dogs ran up to either side of him and licked the palms of his hands. Some of the local surfers hung back, but others, including Eduardo, strolled up to meet the man.

They asked him where he'd come from and he said Puerto Viejo. But later one of the pro-circuit riders who had grown up in Puerto Viejo said he had never seen this guy before at Salsa Brava, or anywhere else on the east coast. Eduardo wasn't a pro, but in ten years he'd surfed Costa Rica from Witch's Rock to down below Dominical, almost to the Panamanian border. He had never seen or heard of this surfer either. Up close, the stranger exuded a sweet, thick scent like almonds and coconuts. When he lifted his hands to his dreadlocks and flung them away from his face, old scars ran down to his wrists. It was impossible to tell his age—his dreadlocks were black as the night sky without a single grey hair, and his skin refused to wrinkle beyond the crease of his eyes squinting in the sunlight. But his eyes were blue, the color of the sky; he seemed to come from the sea.

Eduardo asked him who he was, but the stranger only smiled. Eduardo repeated his question.

"Jesus," the man replied.

"Are you a Rasta, mai?" someone called out.

"What's that?" Jesus answered, squeezing the salt water from his dreadlocks.

The surfers exchanged glances and mumblings with one another, told Jesus con mucho gusto, and praised him for his skills on such powerful surf. Then they headed back up the beach to their parked ATVs, leaving Jesus with his dogs circling and playing. A few of the locals grabbed their boards and hit the waves, this time cutting up and down the faces like knives through guava jelly.

But Eduardo perched atop his four-wheeler and watched Jesus hurling coconuts into the water, the dogs chasing after them. Had the Rasta been telling the truth when he said he'd come from Puerto Viejo? Maybe he was escaping some distant but unforgotten pain, like Eduardo, who had been fourteen when his father abandoned the family. Eduardo, soon after, found his new brotherhood on the beach, one rooted in the physical and the present. The stranger might have once tried to kill himself, survived some kind of accident or knife fight. But did it matter where he'd spent his past? Eduardo didn't sense the man was dangerous.

Eduardo had arrived in Mal Pais not long ago. A few months before, he had suffered a nasty break-up with a half-gringa, half-Tica beach masseuse whom he'd chased from his hometown of Tamarindo down to Manuel Antonio and back again. When that grew tiresome, he'd settled in between in the little dustbowl village of Mal Pais. The name itself meant 'bad country,' although he didn't consider the barreling surf, miles of empty coastline, and stifling, still days too much to bear—at least not yet. But unlike the rest of the surfers, Eduardo wondered how the Rasta Jesus had also ended up in Mal Pais. Was the Rasta Jesus also caught in an in-between , fleeing the condo high-rises that towered over Tamarindo and the crowded tourist beaches of Manuel Antonio? Had he tired of grappling with love like a stubborn snapper at the end of a fishing line, and at last given in to the surf?

The Rasta let out a looping, playful whistle; his dogs retrieved the hairy husks and trotted up the sand. They repeated the ritual and piled them at their master's feet, again and again.

*

By that evening the odd phenomenon of the seemingly otherworldly force that kept everyone but Jesus out of the water had reached the doorways and ears of the community. But everyone knew surfers smoked their share of marijuana; the story was trumped by the more exciting tale of the Rastafarian stranger saving the gringo from drowning. Eduardo, voice raised above the din of his circle, asked if anyone had heard of this happening before, or if someone had a medical background and could explain it. The waitress, setting down a fresh round of beers, smiled and shook her head. Hand on hip, she leaned back and said, "Milagros—don't you believe they can happen? I do."

Don clutched his beer and leaned back. "Or maybe he's about to lead the alien invasion." They laughed.

"So you think," she said, and stepped back. "Maybe he has a special power, this man. God chooses just people to work through."

"If he's some type of alien, mai," someone replied, "he's the kind not interested in abducting any chicks." They laughed.

The waitress laughed back. "Those who choose God lose interest. It's not a bad thing. Just happens."

"Whatever," Don said. "I'm asking around, going to find out who this guy is."

Eduardo nodded, said he'd ask his friends back in Tamarindo. But he didn't like the idea of the Rasta as an ordinary guy, and much preferred to think of him as mysterious and special.

Another day passed, then another, and no one turned up any findings. People kept an eye out for the blue-eyed black man with hair like ropes. No one, at least that Eduardo could see, made any attempts to invite the newcomer to join in for a meal, or just to talk. Eduardo hung back, unsure what to think. Why so much suspicion of this man who had drifted in alone, who showed no malice? Eduardo, too, had come here alone. So why did he hesitate?

For his part, Rasta Jesus, as he came to be known, rarely left the sand. At dawn each day, the Rasta cut across the golden waves with ease, his dreadlocks whipping behind him. Passing by, he wore a relaxed, peaceful expression. At night he camped down the beach, far away from the tiki torch-lit resorts, his driftwood campfire glowing near the place where the jungle waters spilled to the sea, where the crocodiles swam out and hovered off the coast. He had been living on the beach for nearly a month. Eduardo guessed he lived off fish and fruit. The Tica ladies who attended mass every Sunday wondered if the Rasta really might be Jesus Christ, returned to this world at last. But if he was Jesus, why had he come here, to the tip of the Nicoya Peninsula, nearly the end of the earth? And wouldn't he have made himself known by now?

Soon enough another mysterious incident occurred. When a local fishing boat came ashore late one morning, the Rasta leapt out, shouldering a net of wriggling catch. As he trotted briskly toward the main street, the small crew exclaimed to everyone within earshot how the stranger had asked to come along that morning, promising he knew exactly where a school would be passing along the coast, that they would catch more than they ever had.

"I've been fishing these waters all my life, and every year the fish are smaller and their numbers diminish," the captain said. "A record catch today. Where does he come from, this man, that he knows such things?"

At the falafel joint on the main drag, the surfers' other unofficial hangout, Eduardo's little group met for lunch, barefoot and pensive over iced green tea.

"Isn't Jesus supposed to show up in a blaze of glory, with angels blowing trumpets and things?" Don muttered.

"But he's a surfer," Eduardo said. "How is he different from any of us, come here to surf?"

"Listen, mai," said Victor, a Dominican accent hugging his English. "If he's Jesus, he's supposed to be saving the world. But he's out catching fish, and surfing." Victor had been among those who had witnessed the Rasta Jesus' rescue of the gringo. Down his upper arm a tattoo of the Black Madonna wept, her tears splashing onto a radiant Sacred Heart.

Eduardo didn't answer. An iguana zigzagged up a tree; reggae bounced from a corner radio. The Israelis who owned the place—young men like most of the surfers, but with goatees and serious eyes—spoke Hebrew sprinkled with Spanish among themselves one table over. A group of them had moved here from Tel Aviv, tired of watching their friends get blown up in cafés , so they set up a couple of little bungalow hotels and storefronts along the beach. Why come here at all? Was here actually better than anywhere else? Eduardo squinted. Far off down the beach the Rasta Jesus cooked his fish over his campfire. Except for his dogs, he ate alone; Eduardo guessed he had no money, and yet there stood the Rasta, whistling and patting his mutts. A peaceful life.

*

By week's end, the gang of bandidos who had been robbing up and down the peninsula for months resurfaced on the road to the north. Four surfers, two Ticos and two gringos, had their van, boards and wallets stripped from them at gunpoint. The bandidos set up roadblocks and robbed tourists; locals worried they were next. The skeletal police force in the remote parts of the peninsula could do nothing against such teams of criminals with automatic weapons that rivaled their own. Up near Tamarindo, two ornithologists from Stanford University were studying a nest of rare spotted owls in the middle of the night. Residents had mistaken the strangers for bandidos, and the mob nearly beat the two scientists to death.

At the same time, and without warning, the Rasta Jesus began visiting town. He had carved and painted masks out of coco shells and hawked them to tourists, and he cooked and washed dishes here and there—so, like everyone else, he finally could have some money. Eduardo guessed his few weeks of solitude had grown confining, and he was longing for some human interaction. The Rasta became a regular at the bars but never touched a beer, drank only coconut milk. He didn't attend mass or the Shabbat services. Mostly he surfed, and hung out on the edges of Eduardo's circle. The strange phenomenon of the surfing lock-out had not happened again, and most of the surfers began to like and respected Jesus, even if he spoke little. He asked almost nothing of them, but listened, chin in palm, to their stories, seeming to enjoy the company. He surfed the biggest waves, and he could always paddle out no matter how rough the conditions.

Another week or two passed, the town on the cusp of the wet season. Eduardo returned home after a lunch of falafels and mint lemonade to discover his entire bungalow had been cleaned out of valuables. He didn't care about the battered television or the busted six-months-new mini-fridge, but the loss of his three surfboards broke his heart. Saving up for all three had taken him more than half his life. He roared into town on his four-wheeler, dust swirling into his mouth and scratching his eyes, but he didn't stop until he reached the falafel stand. His friends had scattered; no other surfers were hanging out except for Rasta Jesus, drinking his coconut milk and shoveling a pita square with hummus into his mouth. The Israelis were gathered around the end of the table, jabbering in Hebrew. Eduardo started to pull up a chair next to Jesus, but stopped when he realized the Rasta was speaking perfect Hebrew.

Rasta Jesus motioned for him to sit down. "What do you want?" he asked Eduardo, in Spanish.

"You speak Hebrew?" Eduardo asked.

"I speak Spanish, English, Hebrew, yes," Rasta Jesus replied. "You listen, you learn everything around you. Now something has happened to you, and you don't have to tell me what exactly. But you want me to help you?"

Eduardo said nothing. It was the most he'd ever heard Rasta Jesus speak.

"Tacere est consentire," Jesus said. "May I borrow your ATV?"

Eduardo slid over his keys, unsure why he did so. Rasta Jesus sprang up, climbed aboard the four-wheeler, and left Eduardo and the chuckling Israelis behind in a swarm of dust.

Eduardo crept to the middle of the road and stood there with his arms crossed, staring up the bend to the north where the Rasta had disappeared. When Eduardo turned to the men in the falafel café, they only laughed even harder.

"You can kiss those wheels goodbye," one of them said in Spanish.

"I thought maybe he was one of you," Eduardo said.

The Israelis exchanged raised eyebrows and smirks. "Some people pick up languages like other people pick up pens," one of them replied, taking a sip of his coffee. "We have no idea."

Eduardo wandered down to the beach to wait. He lay in one of the hammocks that belonged to a bungalow resort and fell asleep.

He awoke to one of the Rasta's mutts licking his hand. Rasta Jesus was watching him with those blue eyes, squatting atop his ATV, popping almonds into his mouth. Strapped on the back of the ATV were Eduardo's three surfboards. He wondered how the Rasta had found them, but then thought better than to ask. He would only get a riddle in return.

"Thank you so much," Eduardo said. "Surfing is all I know how to do."

"What are you waiting for, mai?" Rasta Jesus said. "Let's go."

Eduardo lent him one of his boards, and the two waded into the water side by side. Although weeks had passed since the Rasta had first appeared in Mal Pais, Eduardo had never gone surfing with him. He had only studied the Rasta's quick elegance from afar. But as the afternoon sun sparkled across the water, Eduardo caught one curling wave after another. Each barrel made him feel as if he might disappear, but he always came out before the wave came down on him and took him under and away from the surface. Later he would think back on the afternoon and remind himself that, yes, this was how the Rasta knew to always be: both inside the world and shut out of it. To know breaks and tides was to know the workings of the universe better than scientists, rabbis, or priests.

Eduardo rocketed out of a tumbling wave—the surf was starting to close out—when he saw the Rasta sprinting on top of the water, his surfboard splashing behind his ankle like a toy. The Rasta, still suspended, scooped up a girl floating face down, just before the Pacific pummeled her into its depths, taking Eduardo under for a bit instead—payback for the good surf.

Even before he reached the shore—and he was paddling fast, arms and shoulders burning—Eduardo saw that he wasn't the solo witness to the Rasta's bending of space. Tourists in sarongs and expensive sunglasses flocked to the spot where the Rasta knelt, attempting to resuscitate the girl. Eduardo pushed them aside.

"He needs room, please," Eduardo begged; the Rasta's dreadlocks shook and he made a shrill humming sound in his throat. Panicked voices in English chopped the humid air: "He's going to kill her," a lady said. "Is this man a doctor?" The thick scent of sunscreen filled Eduardo's throat as he repeated his commands. "He needs air," Eduardo said, but no one heard him. The Rasta was breathing hard, trying to gather enough into his chest, but every time he brought his cupped hands to the girl's gaping mouth, sucked, and spat, only a small amount of water hit the sand.

*

When he appeared in the towns of Mal Pais or Santa Teresa in the days immediately following, people either flocked to Rasta Jesus and grasped his rough hands, begging for him to heal a sick relative or tell them the future, or kept their distance, changed barstools if he sat down next to them. Why was it, they asked, that this man, whom dozens had seen sprint across the water, couldn't succeed in bringing the drowned girl back to life? A few even blamed him for being unlucky. He was bound to cause trouble, they said, and he should leave before he gave the town a worse name.

Days passed and the rains arrived, but the Rasta Jesus remained. He moved off the beach to a maid's room in the back of one of the bungalow hotels, strung hemp necklaces with beads and sold these along with his coco shells. One afternoon Eduardo was riding his

4-wheeler to the falafel stand in the rain when he spotted the Rasta on the side of the road. The Rasta was wearing a giant garbage bag as a poncho and had wrapped his mass of dreads in a plastic bag, too.

"Need a lift?" Eduardo asked.

"Surf, mai," the Rasta said. "Can you take me to Mexico?" He raised a plastic bag, this one heavy as a laundry sack, and stuffed full. Hemp necklaces poked out the gap at the top.

"The rain can't last more than another day or two," Eduardo said. Even as he spoke, he had to shout over the monsoon. "You won't catch a bus coming here 'til the road dries out, anyway."

The Rasta glanced up at the sky, wished Eduardo well, and turned back down the drive toward the bungalow hotel. Eduardo continued down the road, but the mention of Mexico, the one place he hadn't surfed yet in Latin America, stirred something in his heart. He'd heard of the breaks on the Baja Peninsula and near Acapulco. It didn't rain very much up there. On the way he could stop in and visit his mother and siblings.

Eduardo had told the surfers his version of the drowning, plus the prelude of the stolen and retrieved surfboards. That episode won over most of his friends. For some of them, at least, the girl's unhappy end proved one thing—that Rasta Jesus wasn't the Jesus sent to redeem the world after all. But he was a decent individual, though unusual, worthy of their acceptance. Now Eduardo told them about the episode on the road, that the Rasta Jesus looked like he might be leaving for good.

"If he was going to leave, he'd be gone already," Don said. "Any coward can slink out when people start to talk shit, but not Jesus." He winked at the rest of them over the joint he was rolling. "Besides, why would he leave just when he's making friends?"

"No way is he Christ," Victor said. "The real Jesus would have never been able to raise someone from the dead one day and screw it up the next."

"Maybe he just wasn't in the zone," Don said. His tan had faded with the absence of the sun, and white hairs peppered the blonde at his temples. "So he's not the Messiah. So what? He's the best surfer I've ever seen who's never gone pro. Who do you think he is?" Don nudged Eduardo.

"I don't know," Eduardo said. "I hope he sticks around for a while."

The conversation turned to a bet if the rains would stop tomorrow, and then a debate on whether or not to trust the surf report; they wanted to drive over to the Caribbean where Salsa Brava was supposedly going off. Eduardo eyed the map tacked to the wall a few feet away. He had never traveled north of Nicaragua. Maybe he and Jesus could travel together, share stories of all the places they'd gone and people they'd met. He'd be curious to find out what experiences had led the Rasta here, and where he had learned to surf so well. Was it possible Jesus had taught himself? Had the waves saved him, in some way, from a darker path, even if he shirked the tribe he belonged to? Or maybe he had put that path behind him but felt the darkness chasing him, no matter how welcoming his new surroundings—his unwieldy, divine gifts an inevitable source of misunderstanding and conflict? And so best to keep moving on.

When Eduardo left, instead of going home, he headed to the Rasta's quarters, a concrete block room next to the laundry facilities. Rasta Jesus sat on his cot with his board across his lap, waxing quickly, almost feverishly. Eduardo had been leaning in the doorway a full two minutes before the Rasta took notice.

"Rains will be gone overnight," Rasta Jesus said. "Get ready."

"What about Mexico?" Eduardo said.

The Rasta paused. He clucked his teeth and made a quick, knife-slitting gesture across his throat. "Too dangerous," he said. "But that will pass. What's wrong with Mal Pais? Here's not such a bad place, mai." He grinned and waited for Eduardo to answer before returning to his board.

Eduardo stood there, stunned. The room contained nothing but the board, the clothes the Rasta was wearing, and the neat piles of hemp, beads, and coco shells on a tabletop. Fruit flies silently danced atop the mangoes, papayas, and starfruit heaped inside the door. If there was a quieter room apart from the rest of the world, Eduardo couldn't guess. For the first time, he also sensed loneliness—not the Rasta's, but his own, a deep loneliness that had forever driven him to pick up and go, trade his ATV for a van, and pack his bags for the next town. Yet he had never thought of himself as lonely, just restless.

The rains would pour for four more months, the road melting to mud and houses sliding down the hillsides. The big waves would swell, the locals paddling out to ride them. For now Eduardo rode home, his poncho hood down. The rain was falling lighter now, and he laughed as the cool air struck his face.

SUSTAINABLE PRACTICES

COMPANY MISSION

Before takeoff the flight attendants hand out bottled Tahiti Water to everyone in business class. Nina's been longing to go to Tahiti, despite the staggering price of jet fuel driving up ticket costs, the pressure to cut down on small expenses to save for a mortgage, and the wedding. When the time came to book the honeymoon, Nina was adamant. Here was their chance to visit the famous volcanic artesian aquifer as portrayed on the bottle. Clint favored Greece or Italy, someplace with historical ruins, but Nina uploaded the island's official tourism website. Everyone visits Europe, she pleaded. Why not Tahiti?

ECONOMIC CONTRIBUTIONS

While packing, Nina clicked the link titled "Fun Facts" on the website: "We are proud to bring jobs to a part of the world that needs them. Our team works hard to bring each drop from the rock to your lips, to share Earth's pure gift with you." Next, the slide-show. One shot captured a group of brown-faced men in blue work shirts, their smiles bright and arms crossed, a white-walled factory behind them. What else would these islanders do if not for the bottling plant jobs? Would they be better off if they fished, or served on the cruise ships? To her itinerary she added the plant site, a day's trek from their luxury beach hut. They would need to take a local bus—thrilling! She daydreamed hashtags for social media posts: #travelbug, #bucketlist, #traveldeeper, #instalove

TASTE

Clint is reading *The Economist*, Nina the in-flight magazine. Clint says, "No way is that water from Tahiti."

Nina taps the bottle. "They can't claim all this if it isn't true."

"I bet you in a couple of years there'll be news about some scandal. That the water's really from some polluted lake in Arkansas."

Nina drinks, smacking her lips just for spite. She imagines the minerals strengthening her bones, the silica magically spurring her hair and nails to grow.

"And the land next to the lake's been fracked by the nearby refinery."

"Guess I'll have to show you the bottling plant myself."

"What about the volcano?"

"The aquifer," she corrects him, "is underground; the factory sits on top of it. But we can go, I'm sure." She takes another long sip from the bottle.

"Scam," Clint says, fixing on the pages in front of him. "The whole world's going broke, and it's because we're importing water"— he lifts his bottle—"from Tahiti. But whatever makes you happy, baby." She snuggles next to him, Clint's hand stroking her knee.

THE ISLAND

Clint and Nina spend the first three days in Tahiti riding jet-skis and catamarans, sunning and snorkeling, drinking and fucking. He admits, silently and reluctantly, that this is better than the ruins of Pompeii or the Roman Forum. He begins to realize why Gauguin stayed, and hopes Nina has forgotten about the water. But on the fourth day he arrives at the breakfast buffet and finds her asking a hotel clerk about the local bus schedule to the other side of the island to the supposed Famous Volcanic Artesian Aquifer As Portrayed On The Bottle™, tucked away in some lush, pristine, and otherwise undisturbed valley. The clerk, a young native woman in pressed boutique hotel whites, absorbs Nina's questions with a bewildered, strained look. Clint wonders how many nosy American tourists harass the locals about a water-bottling plant belonging to a multinational corporation, if anyone, other than Greenpeace fanatics on their way to chase down whaling ships, or some other type of sandal-recycling liberal. They can go there, but there isn't much to see, the clerk says. "The roads are not good. That part of the island is very remote." Clint shrinks behind his pineapple and sips, the juice sweet, iced perfection. Another day in the sun, a few beers and a firewalker show later that night would be just fine with him.

Nina approaches, waving a colored tourist map marked with the clerk's directions.

ECOSYSTEM

"One billion people worldwide lack clean drinking water," Clint reminds her as they zip shut their day packs. "And I know you don't want to hear this, sweetie, but consumers are nothing more than big kids who believe in fairy tales."

"I read labels," Nina says. "I'm informed."

The bus is packed with islanders; Nina and Clint are the only tourists aboard, squeezed into the last bench seat in the back. Nina sips a Tahiti Water from the resort. The bus winds through the countryside, the air humid and choked with diesel, the mood solemn despite the Christmas songs belting from the speakers: a Kenny Rogers/Dolly Parton album Nina recalls from when she was a girl.

They pass concrete block dwellings. One woman stands outside beating a rug. Several others hang laundry. Mutts chained to trees bark and lurch at the road. Once in a while, a multi-storied house with lots of glass looms from the hills overhead, the driveway and property barricaded by a gate, shiny European SUVs parked in front.

There have been heavy rains in the valley, and when they stop in one of the towns the bus's tires spin in the mud and the driver shoos everybody out, jabbing his thumb toward the stand on the adjacent corner. Nina clutches her backpack and slips her hand into Clint's. They join the throng of islanders, abandon the bus stuck in the street. No one says anything. Even passengers riding together remain silent, so Nina and Clint do too. Under a shabby lean-to they await the bus for the volcano. Half of the passengers seem to decide to walk wherever they are going, and soon become dots beneath the sugarcane. Nina sips her water. She snaps a picture of her feet in pink flip-flops with the little strawberry insignia on them, her pedicure still intact from the wedding (#perfectpedi #honeymoon #daytrip #lovinglife), tries to upload to her newsfeed, but fails. No connection. She stares at the brown feet of the woman next to her, the long hard toenails in cracked, nameless plastic thongs, and puts away her phone.

THE AQUIFER

Nina and Clint hike down into the valley with nothing but cows and fruit farms on either side. The Tahiti Water plant comes into view. They approach the entrance. Signs in French, English, and Tahitian, and an armed guard greet them.

The guard gestures to the white, windowless building behind him that somewhat resembles an airplane hangar. One of his dark-blue sleeves reads SECURITY in white letters. His other arm cradles an automatic rifle. Clint wonders how many locals read English, but the gun does the job. When Nina steps forward, the guard's grip drops to the barrel. He gives a curt headshake, says, "My apologies. Visiting hours are closed because of recent unrest, *vous comprenez?*" He speaks English with a French accent.

"Unrest?" Nina looks around at the desolate two-lane road. In the field opposite, cows lie underneath the palms, blinking at the buzzing flies. Clint inhales manure. She says, "You've got to be kidding me."

SUSTAINABLE PRACTICES / 43

"Please, madam." The guard is not smiling. His face behind the mirrored shades glistens with sweat. "There is nothing for you to see, just bottles filling up with water, I promise. If you go up the road, a bus should come in another hour."

"We know," Nina interrupted. "The bus just dropped us off. We've been on two buses already to get here and walked the last kilometer, and your website says there's a tour. I want to speak to a manager." She charges ahead, past the sign that reads, in three languages, WORKING FACTORY. EMPLOYEES ONLY BEYOND THIS POINT.

"You can't go in there, madam," the guard calls and darts ahead to block her. He raises the gun but stops short of pointing it.

"We're going. *Pas probleme, d'accord?*" Clint says loudly, raises his hands palms-up. The guard lowers the rifle, saunters back a few paces nearer to his booth. Clint steers Nina by the elbow to the road.

"The website said daily tours." Nina shakes her head. She breaks away, clutching the shoulder straps of her backpack. "Everything online said so." She removes her sunglasses, wipes her eyes with the back of one hand. The desolate valley is thick with vegetation, the pavement scalding. Clint wishes for a shower, then a nap in the A/C.

UNTOUCHED BY MAN

They hike back to the village where the second bus dropped them off. Thirsty, shins aching, they duck into an open storefront advertising Coca-Cola from a dingy, swinging sign. Clint asks for a Diet Coke, Nina her usual Tahiti Water. The Tahitian woman behind the counter, middle-aged, her hair hidden in a flower-print wrap, removes the caps of both bottles, sets them down. Clint pays.

Nina guzzles the bottle's contents so hard the plastic crackles. The cartoon-like graphic of the volcano with a miniature Tahiti Water bottle sprouting up and floating in the clouds like the assumption of a saint merges with the actual volcano in clear view behind them.

"You should be enjoying the beaches, with a coconut drink," the woman says in island-accented English. "The valley is too hot."

Nina mentions the website's claim to offer factory tours, but the woman stares blankly. She doesn't own a computer. "The only white people allowed are the ones who come in jeeps, the bosses from California."

Clint says, "Lots of people around here must work for the company."

The woman nods, wipes down the counter. A teenage Tahitian boy glides up on a bicycle, hops off and orders something in their language. The woman carves up a pineapple, drops the chunks into a blender. She reaches beneath the counter, turns on a faucet. Then lifts a glass sloshing with brown-tinged water. She holds it up to the sunlight. Tiny dirt particles dance and settle. She tosses out the contents, splashes some bottled Tahiti Water into the blender. The blades churn a pineapple blizzard. #fairtrade #shoplocal #island-heaven #sustainability

ABOUT THE WATER

Back on the bus they are quiet and sleepy. Nina dreams of being chased by a great snake in the Tahitian jungle. The snake wants to swallow her whole, but she is running, determined to outlast him. Finally she finds a hollow tree and hides inside.

Clint sleeps in patches. His dreams mix with the jolts and fumes and the low island voices. He and Nina are back on the valley road in front of the bottling plant. Somehow they break in. They reach the center of the dark, vast warehouse and the aquifer, a rusty spigot dripping brown water. The squeaky footsteps of the guards approach, and they flee. They reach a ridge and peer down into a crater. But instead of lava rocks the crater is filled with Tahiti Water bottles.

EDUCATION

The next morning Nina is gone. They are booked on a catamaran cruise. In the bathroom she has left a note on hotel stationary: "Couldn't sleep so did some Googling in lobby. Guess what? Big local protest today in front of the Tahiti Water office in the harbor. Knew you'd try and talk me out of it. Hope you'll join me." Her cell phone and charger are gone, but neither of them get reception here. What the hell is she doing? Clint fumes as he tugs on shorts and a shirt. Why does she insist on carrying out this Nancy Drew stint, when he's told her time and again the truth—that this company's eco-happy spin is a capitalist front like all the others. Only she doesn't read the same underground media that he does, won't admit the extent the Tahiti Water private security may go to in dispersing the crowd.

He skirts past the front desk on his way out. "Would you please do me a favor and cancel that catamaran cruise we've got booked today?" he says. "And by the way, did you see my wife leave early this morning?"

"No, sir, I'm afraid I just started my shift—but wait, sir." The clerk stoops to grab something from behind her desk, then darts after him, holding up a frosty bottle of Tahiti Water. "Care for a water to take with you, sir? Complimentary, of course. We don't want our guests to get light-headed."

The hotel is in an isolated, picturesque cove, hardly close to the industrial waterfront of Papeete. Clint hails a cab, orders the driver to bring him to the water protests. The driver pretends not to know what Clint is talking about until Clint threatens to get out and take another taxi. Morning traffic jams the winding two-lane road, and diesel exhaust chokes the air. The minutes tick by. They pass the harbor of container ships, shantytowns climbing the slopes above Papeete, round another bend, and then hit the protest. It's mid-morning. Police in riot gear face off with the crowd of demonstrators—hundreds, maybe a thousand—in front of a half-constructed complex, a warehouse like the one in the valley but adjoined by administrative offices. The police wield their riot shields awkwardly, half-hiding behind them; the officers appear uncertain and intimidated by the shouting throng. Clint jumps out, instructing the driver to wait, and races into the crowd searching for Nina. Signs block him from every angle: "BOTTLED WATER FOR A FEW = BROWN WATER FOR MANY" and "Everyone has a right to CLEAN, FREE WATER." A whistle blasts and the crowd surges, hurling dozens of empty Tahiti Water bottles through the air; the hollow plastic pelts Clint's head and back. Then comes more shouting and a hissing sound, the crowd yelling and dispersing. Clint's eyes water. He thinks: *So, I've just been tear-gassed by Tahitian police in French riot gear on my honeymoon, and I can't find my wife.*

The factory whistle blares again. Staggering, Clint sights a pale woman in shorts bent over in the parking lot, hands pressed to her thighs, gasping. The pink flip flops. He runs to her. Nearby, management workers in blue company shirts and khakis stream from the buildings, escorted by the Tahiti Water company's private security guards. The guards outnumber the bewildered, skittish police. A passing worker frowns, eyeing the chaotic panorama of crushed signs and bottles, the protesters now hunkered in small groups, choking and wiping their watery faces. Some of the employees load pallets of Tahiti Water into their Japanese and French cars and drive away.

Clint rubs his face with his t-shirt, eyes stinging from tears and sunscreen, and tear gas. Nina chokes down a sob. He folds her to his chest, steers her toward the idling taxi. #bethechange #honeymoon #activistlife #occupywater #tahitiwatertruth #tahitiwatersucks

SUSTAINABLE PRACTICES

For the last four days they towel off, read books on their Kindles, and sip tropical drinks. They laugh and talk of the future, about freedom within commitment. Clint wants to blog, exposing Western businesses with idealist facades that take advantage of the Third World; Nina wants to enroll in an online university course called "Reporting from Afar: Journalism in the Age of Social Networking and the Internet." Maybe they will one day write a book together.

But as the flight takes off from Papeete the squabbling begins— surely just the #newlyweditch for #healthyalonetime. The flight attendant passes out what will be #Ninaslasttahitiwater. She and Clint clasp hands until Tahiti is no more than a brown dot in the shimmering blue, the #scaryprotest already a #lousysidetrip inside an otherwise #perfectescape.

ARTHUR AND GEORGE: THE VOYAGE BEGINS

When I found a lump in my right ball I knew I needed to tell George, but first I needed to find a new job. Maybe at one of those upscale grocery stores, working in the deli or sushi bar—didn't matter to me, just as long as the health insurance was decent. On my breaks I'd sit out back on the greasy steps and make calls. Days off, I'd secretly put on my chef jacket and fill out applications at every Whole Foods, Trader Joe's, and Costco within biking distance. Years with no health insurance and no dentist, and I had the bad teeth and blood pressure to show for it. Even at a chain I'd probably have to wait ninety days or something for the full benefits to kick in. You don't live to forty-six and stay stupid—that crotch-marble meant cancer. I had no family, no girlfriend, just my friend George, a victim of chronic social anxiety, but undiagnosed.

The day after I found the marble George didn't show up to open at work. Fourteen years in that kitchen and George had never even been late, so I knew he was in trouble. George hadn't said anything about quitting. He hadn't said anything about anything. He cooked and worked dish, now and then he threw pots and pans when a server pissed him off, but he didn't talk much. Never did. The only phone he had was a landline. The manager and I called him. We tried him twice that morning, and again after the lunch rush. "Pick up," I muttered.

All I could think was that somebody had broken into George's apartment, robbed him, left him unconscious or dead. The closest guy I had to a brother.

By then I was pretty freaked out. I needed to go check on him, but he lived down 436 by the Orlando airport, a good thirty minutes from Winter Park, way too far for me to ride my bike. I called the night cook to come in early. If anything I should have gone right to the Urgent Care, my ass warming the plastic seat, waiting to see a doctor.

Instead I took the bus and to George's apartment.

I knocked and called out a few times before he jerked open the door. He hadn't shaven in a few days and the stubble, greyish-white, grazed his jaw. I'd always thought him a fairly attractive man—he was no Paul Newman or anything, but he had that chiseled face, medium build, and all-American look. Whereas I had the beady black eyes and wiriness that the wrestling coach was after, way back at Blue Ridge High. Wrestling was big in Pennsylvania among the coal-miners. My pops had been both a wrestler in high school and forty years a miner, and his old coach hounded after me to hit the mats. But we'd wanted none of that, me and George—no grappling for points, no chanting at pep rallies for some lame "school spirit," no hours spent in cold shafts underground, blasting and digging for lumps of soot. We'd met in English class and hit it off over the Tolkien unit , the only ones who checked out the rest of the series after *The Hobbit* from the library. All around us was gloom, dirty slush, and bigots, and why live among that? Dwarves, we called the miners. Not me. Why not go somewhere where you could have year-round sun, a warm breeze, and a backyard with all the oranges you could eat—like Kerouac did, and the rest of the Beats?

"A new start," I said one day, "in a far off land. That's just what we need." He nodded in silence. It was the morning after some jocks from our school had recognized him at the local Renaissance Faire, in a costume he'd made himself from old feed sacks. We were thick as thieves that summer, me and George, and I was supposed to go too but had just started my first job and got called in to flip burgers. The jocks beat him up pretty good, sent George to the ER with cracked ribs and a concussion. I'd always thought of the decision as mutual, but I was the one who started talking Florida at graduation.

Standing there before me now, my friend wasn't looking so hot. Stale breath and unclipped nails will do that to you.

"No call, no show," I said, leaning in. "Never done that before. What's up?"

"Sorry." He squinted into the sunlight. "Must have turned the ringer off and forgot."

"You sick? Why didn't you call in?"

"I'm not sick," he said sharply. His adamant tone took me by surprise. "I don't know what's wrong. Just need some rest. I don't know if I can go back and work the line." He rubbed his eyes and I crept farther into the apartment, looking around.

The place certainly smelled the same: old soup, faint mildew, laundry detergent. Clutter everywhere. But a few things struck me as odd. Next to George's computer desk, his *Civilization* games and *Lord of the Rings* collector figurines, stood a tower of books on money. *The Mindset of a Millionaire, The Investor Next Door, Visualize and You Shall Reap*—a whole bunch of titles like that. Pieces of colored paper and bookmarks stuck out crookedly from between the pages. George never mentioned anything about money; we stuck to punk music and Middle Earth, memories of happier times, when rent was dirt cheap and we spent our weekends at shows.

George dialed work. As he held for the manager, I could hear the drunken laughter of the bar regulars and the clang of registers and silverware. When the manager got on George apologized for not calling sooner. He told her he'd been having chest pains. She told him to not mess around and to get checked out.

"Chest pains? Why didn't you tell me?" I asked as soon as he hung up. George had experienced these symptoms before, a byproduct of his anxiety. "Let's go then. I think I can manage to drive you to the ER." I didn't have a car, but George did—a little banger of a Honda.

"Nope, I'll go myself."

"And why the hell would you do that? What if they check you in?"

"I have my reasons," he said, chin lifted. "And I know what you're up to."

"What are you talking about? Up to what? I'm here, checking on you. Now let's go to the ER."

"Quit it!" He stamped his palm on the counter, sent skidding a recipe print-out: *Savory Favorites of the South Seas.* "I've seen you riding the back streets in your chef coat. Why do you all of a sudden want to cook somewhere else?"

I unwound the Walkman headset from around my neck, hoping he didn't notice how my hands shook. "Just sick and tired of rolling burritos, I guess. Do I need a better reason? You don't have to stay there, either."

He kept silent—stewing, I could tell, by his set jaw and the way he curled and straightened his fingers. I thumped his shoulder twice, flung open the door, and said, "Okay, then. Let me know the stress test results."

So I boarded the bus, more uneasy than when I'd arrived, and blasted the Ramones' "We're a Happy Family"—one of our favorite songs from back in the day. So far I wasn't feeling anything else wrong down there, but we were older now, getting to the point where everything starts breaking down. What about George? What if these weren't his run-of-the-mill pangs, and he was about to have a massive heart attack any minute? I could barely take care of myself, which is maybe why I've always hung back at making more friends, at least the close kind. Too much responsibility. I felt like I was having one of the work nightmares I get sometimes after a busy weekend: the kitchen slammed, a dozen orders fluttering across the line. But for some reason I was cooking by myself, drowning in tickets and fryer grease. The whole ride back to Winter Park I kept on my shades, avoided the glances of the other passengers and stared out the window. I'd get to the clinic on my next day off, I told myself, although part of me didn't want to go. Until then worrying wouldn't change anything, and if I had to worry I'd rather get to the bottom of what was wrong with my friend. Is this how you become an old man? I wondered. If you're lucky enough to live that long.

*

The next day after the lunch rush I called George and suggested we meet at the Thai place, our longtime spot in the Stein Mart plaza. Getting out will do you good, I insisted, then asked how he was feeling. He'd spent the morning at the doctor's office but refused to tell me anything more over the phone. I got there at five-thirty, ordered a Singha. I was almost through with my beer when George lumbered in. He frantically circled before the hostess stand, looking lost until I waved him over. I asked about his diagnosis. The doctor found him to be one-hundred-percent healthy, with the exception of his ten-pound beer paunch and a couple of infected toenails. "And I don't know if I'm coming back to work," he said proudly.

"But the doctor found nothing wrong," I said.

"That doesn't mean I'm all right. Whatever those pains were in my chest, they were real. And you know what?"

He brought out a map and unfolded it right over our dumplings and summer rolls. This was no kiddie-map, but the detailed professional kind with the elevations, wide as the booth. The creases were all split white, so he must have been obsessing over this thing for longer than I wanted to guess. He started yakking about adventurers: Indiana Jones, Jason and the Argonauts, Coronado, Shackleton. How we spend all this time fantasizing about other worlds when the ruins of entire civilizations we barely know anything about are right here—ruins as plain as the dumplings on our plates. "I get too stressed over that printer spitting out orders," he said. "It never stops. And working dish, same thing. Those chest pains are the sign that I need to give up the kitchen. Follow my dream."

"Your dream?" I echoed skeptically.

"Well, maybe not my dream," he stammered, "but *a* dream, at least."

Did he really expect me to buy this? First off, George liked to blame the kitchen for his temper tantrums and silent frenzies when the real cause was his lifelong paranoia, triggered by the ex-con line cooks and stoned servers screwing up orders and talking back. This was also the most I'd heard George speak in one stretch since his mother's funeral. Except for a couple of stepsiblings and cousins up north he had no family, and he wasn't exactly good at keeping in touch. Like George, I had a few cousins back in PA, probably riding ATVs and flying high on meth. Otherwise I had no siblings, my parents both dead.

"I want to go on a quest," he said. "A real one."

The only quest I'd ever seen George attempt was to fetch tamales in the walk-in. "I thought you loved cooking," I said. "I'm close to landing another job. Maybe we can work at a new place together."

"Nah, I don't want to work, or go back to school, or volunteer. Don't you ever think about death, Artie? How you could spend your whole life in drunk Poppy's kitchen and miss out on everything? When your life could've been more like," he paused, gaze lifted, "like *Shōgun?*"

A dated poster of a gold reclining Buddha staring blankly hung overhead—a Thai Air advertisement for Bangkok. "You've got money in the bank," I said flatly. "I need to find a job. With decent benefits, maybe even a retirement plan."

"You can't work forever." His tone sometimes goes into this know-it-all sing-song that I find irksome. "I know you only like fiction, but maybe you should read up on how to invest."

By then I was fuming, speechless. The waitress delivered our plates and he dug in.

"Something wrong with your food?" he asked, his eyebrows knitting a scraggly 'w.'

"Easy to talk about a vacation when you've got a nice fat cushion," I said, clutching my fork. "And that's what this quest idea is—a vacation. Hell, go for it. I'm surprised you're not on Easter Island right now."

George chewed slowly. He has this way of staring at you as if he's still a little kid. "You feeling okay lately, Artie?" he said. "Is there something you're hiding from me?"

"Absolutely not," I said, adjusted my seat, and ate. "You don't need to worry about me. If you're wondering why I'm looking for a better job, I guess I just want a change of scenery. Some of us don't have the luxury of not working for a living, is all."

George shoved his plate and beer aside. "So stubborn," he said. "You know, maybe you're right. What I'm talking about, maybe this isn't your kind of thing. So forget it." He yanked out the plastic baggie he used to hold his cash and peeled off a bill.

"Oh, yeah? Well, look around sometime," I said, leaning in. "Adventures are for college kids and rich people."

"You could join the Peace Corps. We both could, right now."

"That's nice but I've got things I need to take care of before I go running off to live in a mud hut." The waitress dropped off our check and the take-out boxes, and I paused. I usually give my extras to George since he hates to cook at home and will otherwise live off soup and deli sandwiches. But before I could he bolted up and slammed his chair into the table so hard that my remaining beer sloshed onto my t-shirt.

"Changing your attitude, that's free," he said. He crushed his map to his chest, hastily folded it. "We're running out of time, but it's up to you to choose. It's like you've given up, and I almost had too—I didn't know how close I was until I woke up the other day. Maybe that's why I got those chest pains. But I'm telling you, Artie, I can't do it anymore." He headed for the door.

I picked up the ten dollar bill he left, not even enough to cover half his order. Typical. He hadn't looked at the price column of a menu in the ten years since his mom passed away, when he found out he didn't have to rely on his paycheck.

Nonsense, was all I could think while pedaling home, a medium-rare dusk hugging the sky . That's what this whole lousy falling out business amounted to. But where had this come from, and why now? What buried grudges simmered underneath this mess? Were we on the brink of a permanent blow-up? Was that even possible? What no one else knew about George was that his mother left him a ton of stocks and mutual funds, plus her property up in Pennsylvania. He could live off that nut anytime, had just chosen not to—up until this spat he'd acted embarrassed about having money. But he knew what I took home every payday, never mentioned these investment books of his or offered a loan. Easy to take off on some outrageous quest if you've got a nest egg. And to save your life. That was one thing George couldn't deny. No way did I want to tell him, have him think he owed me anything.

At thirteen George and I became blood brothers. We had built model airplanes together, swapped books, helped each other get over girlfriends stomping on our hearts and moving out, found each other cheap apartments. Maybe by dreams George meant something different—not what you invent alone but what you can only experience with somebody else. As men without wives, without families, almost to fifty, what does that mean?

Hours after our argument at the Thai restaurant, I was still pacing and fuming. I hate to admit it, but I've got tendencies to obsess over routines myself. After our weekly dinner out, George would come over to my place and we'd play chess on my Special Edition Tolkien set. That night I secretly hoped that he would call me first and apologize for storming out of dinner, but then thought about how his chest pains, real or not, had weirded him out. He wasn't going to call. I missed him already. Last week we'd stumbled upon an old Gilliam flick on late-night cable and laughed ourselves silly. Few mortals are so simply entertained.

So I called. He answered and right away apologized for how he left the table. But when I invited him over, he breathed into the phone for a solid minute. Then said, "Sorry, I've got plans."

"Plans?" I squeaked, rejection welling in my throat.

"I'm actually going to check out the Orlando Fencing Club. They meet Monday nights at the downtown Y. Want to come?"

I pictured a too-bright gymnasium, pockets of strangers, awkward introductions. And what about the lunges? There I'd be, lurching and stumbling in agony over my scrotum. Which I'd mostly succeeded in ignoring, except that just since dinner it had grown more swollen. "That's not really my thing," I told him.

"We could use some more friends, Artie. A community."

"What are you, a Communist?" No reply. The dense discomfort in my groin seemed to crawl up my leg and into my gut. I saw clearly the days ahead: clocking my hours, biking home sticky with fajita juice and drained, until I got too sick to work anymore. I said, "Maybe you can bring me one of those investment books tomorrow."

"Sure. You okay?" He fumbled with something, and the next second it clattered upon the tile but he didn't miss a beat. "I still really think you should come. Where else you gonna find swashbuckling, and for free?"

"But why fencing? Why not just come over and we'll do our usual. Pick up some Rolling Rock, find an old B-movie."

"Nope, gotta get moving. My doctor said I sit around too much. Need more physical fitness. You could, too, Artie. Don't think I haven't noticed"—here my stomach dropped—"you haven't been looking so hot."

"Now you're really dreaming. I'm fine, fit as a fiddle."

"Whatever you say. Last chance. I'm happy to come pick you up."

Why did he keep insisting? Why didn't I just tell him about my ball? *Thwack, thwack* trilled the sound on the other end; he huffed, swore. That was when I realized what he'd been doing—trying out fencing moves, probably with an umbrella or yardstick. Fencing, where had this come from? Did I really not look well, or was he just bluffing?" My heart thudded harder.

"Thanks," I said quietly. "I'm sure you'll have fun. But I just don't feel like it."

I clicked off, chucked the phone hard at the couch.

*

Someone knocked at my door after midnight. Alarmed but mostly pissed off, I popped up from the couch. No remedy for life hitting the toilet like zoning out on old Star Trek and bad habits, like smoking cloves. Hesitantly, I opened the door. George barged in, backpack overflowing—a compass dangled from one clip, a beaded-and-feathered amulet we'd made in Eagle Scouts from another.

He said, "Just stopped to say goodbye and drop off some food. Only room for packaged goods where I'm heading." He chucked a Ziploc of cold cuts my way, which I barely caught.

"Where's that?" I tried not to sound worried.

"If I told you, you'd have to come along," he replied stiffly.

"What about your place?" I frowned. "You can't just leave."

"My stepsister's coming down next week. She'll pack it up in storage."

I darted to the mini-fridge for a Rolling Rock, offered one— maybe I could stall him. He held up a palm, Buddha-like. My skin flushed, head-to-toe. "So you're just going to bug out, is that it? Not even have a beer, tell me where you're going, how long you'll be gone—two weeks, four weeks. Forever." I kicked shut the fridge door, tore off the bottle cap. He stood, pouting, lip frozen in place. "You can't just leave and not tell anyone where you're going. That's crazy. People disappear forever like that. Remember Randy Motts?" He'd been in our graduating class. Couple of years ago, word trickled down from PA that he'd been living in San Miguel de Allende for a while. He sent a letter to a bunch of folks back home that he was going off alone into the desert, something about reuniting with his "divine self." No one ever heard from him again. That was seven years ago.

George shook his head. "Nope, Randy Motts was a burned-out crackpot. Here, you can check my bags. No peyote." He patted himself down, smiling, chin lifted.

Packages of mac and cheese and marshmallows spilled out of his bag's top flap, and maps jutted from the side pockets of his cargo shorts, along with a printed ticket of some sort—to where? I took a swig of beer, then another, and my chest tightened. Dinners alone at the Thai place on nights off, calling an Uber or taxi to bring me to doctor's appointments, hospitals, maybe chemo. The A/C unit was silent but I shivered. "Okay, take me with you," I said evenly. "I might even have a better shot at a job somewhere else."

"A man's quest is his own." George backed toward the door. "You will find your own path, brother." He bolted into the darkness. The screen door floated shut behind him.

"Wait," I cried, but the right words clogged my throat. I raced down the porch steps. George flicked on his headlights. I blurted, "I've got cancer in my balls!"

But too late. He was backing out. Gone.

Three decades, and George was never more than a phone call away. In no more than thirty seconds, I was utterly alone. Why had I always pictured him being there? Because I'd never fathomed myself leaving him? Was I still that childish, that immature and naïve? A decade ago and in the final months before her lungs quit I'd promised George's mom I'd look out for him, since we both pretty much knew he'd never get married. That was the last time both George and me had gone back to PA. I couldn't afford to; he could afford to, but didn't.

I stood beneath the live oaks, tree frogs chirping and the traffic off 17-92 whooshing by. For the first time in my adult life, I had to ask myself: who am I, without this person? How was I going to go on? Just me.

Back inside I fixed up a washcloth with ice cubes, pressed it against my swollen crotch. I felt lightheaded, like I'd never been so awake. Adrenaline high, plus fear. The marble seemed bigger. What if I'd waited too long? Was I pressing against death?

I remembered how catching a trout used to feel, how pumped I used to be after hearing a killer set. Weren't there other ways to live? Maybe we could work in a greenhouse someplace, or for the groves, sorting oranges? I peeled off my skinny jeans and socks, climbed into bed. What had happened to me, the kid who first suggested to Goonball George that we become blood brothers? "For life," I had said. Probably was reading too many Stephen King novels back then. God knows I'd watched *Easy Rider* one too many times. I should have been scared of getting beaten up—I'm still a puny runt—but back then I pretended so much that I was one of the mouthy Sex Pistols that nobody had any doubt I was wild and badass, including me. No one bothered George after what happened at the Renaissance Faire, once we became a unit. Where, now, had my wild heart gone?

And I suppose I could have more friends. But I don't care for the company of most other people—the petty, ordinary conversion, and keeping up of social graces. Takes a long time to get past that, and know someone on the level I know George. When he does open his mouth, you can never guess what he's going to say. Oh, sometimes I met up with other guys from the kitchen for a movie or a beer, and a few even came over and listened to scratchy records. But nothing clicked. Is it enough that a person has only one friend, if that person is a soulmate of sorts, of genuine and loyal character? Is it okay to look out for someone, more than that person is capable of looking out for you? Somehow I had gotten so used to looking out for George over the years, I'd forgotten about myself. Why didn't I check out a chess club, or a clerk job at a record store, or bar-back somewhere that had live bands, someplace where misfits like me hung out—did

I feel like that would be a betrayal somehow, if I found those things with other people? I had tried with women, had girlfriends here and there, but even the one I met at a punk show didn't stick around after a couple of years. What had happened? At some point I gave up. Too many years with my eye on the fryer basket waiting for the shoestrings to float. The printer screeches, roll a burrito. Wake up the next day, clock-in, repeat. Always broke.

That night I dreamed I'd turned my rented bungalow into a shop— the airplane models, dusty collectible glass, and even my prized albums, all for sale. I'd even given away my cat.

*

A week later, I started a new job at a breakfast place, corporate, with decent benefits and no drunk bar customers demanding special requests for their carne asada and buffalo wings. Thirty days frying eggs, and I'd be covered to see a doctor. Each afternoon when I came home at four I blackened in a square on my calendar. Two weeks passed, and I heard nothing from George. Then one afternoon I clocked out to find I had a bunch of messages, all from him. He'd hopped a freighter and sailed around South America to the Port of Long Beach, but he hadn't accounted for the rolling ocean feeding his claustrophobia and panic attacks. And the ports he'd never have guessed how vast and confusing they were! The day they docked in Mexico he got lost in the yard and almost didn't find his way back to the ship. By the end of the message string, his voice had cracked. Between the gasps I just made out his location, a state park in southern California. I called back and told him to wait there until I arrived, even if it took me until payday to afford the trip. He promised to pay me back, help me out any way he could. "You have every right not to show up," he said. "You've got real worries, sure don't need me around."

Click.

I dumped cat food and water into two large bowls, threw a few changes of clothes, headphones and cassettes into a duffel bag, the whole time squeezing the phone between my ear and shoulder, the marble more painful than ever, telling my new manager that I had a family emergency with my brother and could she please give me a few days?

"What's a few?" she asked.

"A week?" I asked, and gulped.

She grumbled good luck and sorry about my brother.

At the Greyhound station I bought a ticket to San Diego. Only after we'd been on the road for a couple of hours and merged back on the highway at Gainesville did it sink in that I'd probably lost my new job after only three weeks. How quickly I could land another one, full-time, with as good of a healthcare plan, was anyone's guess. Once I found George, I'd ask straight out if he'd help pay for my treatment. After I got him calmed down and thinking clearly again, he'd probably give me hell for not telling him the truth a month ago. It didn't matter. He knew he owed me big time. And I owed him. I had been a jackass not to tell him about my trouble, and an even bigger jackass by having been a drag on our friendship for so long. I just wanted him back safe.

On the flat stretches of highway I skimmed my wilted copy of *Hell's Angels*, a perfect read for my first-ever California trip. You'd think I would have gotten out to the West Coast once by now. For the first time I stopped partway through, didn't bother to dog-ear the page. All these years, maybe I should have been living more like my gonzo hero rather than just devouring his accounts. You gotta admire George for that. I sneezed; the yellowed pages stunk of mildew and dust. I wasn't in the mood for Hunter's voice, either. Probably time to find some new reads for my shelf.

Five cramped days I spent on the Greyhound. The coach reeked of stale body odor and tuna fish. Plenty of time to wonder what a voyage by cargo ship would have been like instead. But taking to the high seas in no way appealed. Once I reached San Diego I took another bus, and at the last stop hitched a ride from a local to the park entrance. The little entrance booth stood empty, and I took a piss on a giant cactus. The marble had increased from dime-sized to nickel. What may kill us, in the end, is what we're most unable or unwilling to confront—the needs we fail to stick up for, the hard questions we fail to ask. As I climbed down a path along the bluffs a breeze billowed George's tent—the same tent we'd used to camp in the Poconos as Eagle Scouts. He'd pitched it as close to the entrance as possible. Unshaven and sunburned as a copper pot, he bent over an old charcoal grill. Chicken and vegetables were ready to roast on rough skewers he'd made from sticks.

"Hey, Prince Caspian," I called into cupped hands. "What're you doing out here?"

George chucked his fork. He jogged over and scooped me in a tight hug. "I can't make it on my own," he muttered, "I tried." He was in the same clothes he'd been wearing the night he left, and my nostrils curled at the first whiff of his funk. Had he been living in this ratty skater band shirt for a month? "This whole being a millionaire thing is worthless."

"Listen, man," I said. "I just got this job where I have no friends. Zero, none. It's scary as hell. In fact, I might already be fired." Which was all I could manage because my throat had gone all tight, as if someone had slapped a collar on it.

"I'm just so sorry. I can't believe I made you come out here like this."

"Hey, no problem. I'm having an adventure, right? California." I gulped air, so stunningly dry, and salt. "I'm fine."

"Are you? You taking care of yourself?" He squinted at me. "You know what I'm talking about."

"Yeah," I said, and shifted my weight. "But how do you know about it? About my sore ball. I haven't told a soul."

"It's your ball?" His eyes grew wide, and his mouth twisted. "I just overheard you on the phone out back one day, when you were on break. You were getting advice from some pharmacist, promised them you'd go in right away. Didn't sound good. Figured you'd tell me when you wanted to."

I nodded, described my symptoms. He brightened. "Doesn't sound like cancer. From where you're describing it, sounds like you may have this thing I once had. Just inflammation. Goes down in a few weeks. But you should probably get checked out just in case."

"Definitely. Well, that's a relief." The stars glittered overhead, the water fading to violet and waves rushing beneath. "Thanks."

I went to the restroom to wash up, came back and handed the soap to George, who cleaned up and changed into one of my tees. I was glad I'd brought an extra sweatshirt. He offered me a swig from a warm bottle of Cuervo Gold. I took one sip, set the bottle on a rock beside our Scout manual, the corners slightly torn but well intact. My copy I must have lost ages ago but George kept an eye on things, when he found them to hold their value. The sun slipped beneath the Pacific. Finite time, boundless space. We'd have to figure out how to book passage, where to go next. And after we dealt with my ailing ball, I'd have to find work. Maybe on a farm somewhere, one of those organic ones. Plant lettuce, spread manure. But I felt like I'd met God, or been enlightened by the desert, because I was free from everything, even as George doddered at arm's length. Somehow I'd made my own mix-tape of myself: the new me and the kid I used to be, always was. The meat sizzled golden brown, smoke billowing and the air scented with pine. I slid my headphones over my ears and smiled. George flipped the chicken, and over the sand for a tablecloth, spread his map.

THE PERFECT PANTRY

Pure vanilla extract, Martha writes. Dutch process-cocoa powder. Italian plum tomatoes, green and black olives, olive paste. Anchovies, anchovy paste, capers, chickpeas, mustards. Italian oil-packed tuna, low-sodium chicken broth. Oils: olive, toasted sesame, truffle. Canned fruits, chutneys, fruit jam, preserves, pickles, artichokes, and relishes. Assorted pasta: spaghetti, penne, rigatoni, fettuccine, lasagna, orzo, couscous. Flours: unbleached all-purpose white and whole wheat. Quick-cooking polenta, stone-ground cornmeal, long grain brown and basmati rice. Black-eyed and split peas, black, pinto, and cannellini beans, green lentilles du Puy. Pine nuts, almonds, hazelnuts, currants, dried apricots, dates, and figs. Vinegars: aged balsamic, red and white wine. Pure maple syrup, molasses, cane sugar, and honey. Sea salt, Himalayan and Celtic. Surely there must be more. Martha refreshes the webpage of the ebullient chef, who is as famous for her retro outfits as her cuisine, and produces her own show on the Food Network. Martha watches the channel every day, since she's barely employed and her modest alimony barely covers the household expenses and health insurance; she must cook more of her meals at home now. She opens another browser, types PANTRY LIST, pen poised above her tablet.

New results, but from sites she doesn't recognize. She clicks on the top link, "Preppers Guide to Food Storage," from a site called

MerryPreppers. "Your prepper's pantry will be the building block of your family's survival system," the page begins. "Have you read our guide, '37 Items to Hoard Before a Crisis'? If so, the list below of essentials to stockpile will likely be familiar to you." Martha has not read the guide, and she's no stranger to crisis. But this was a different kind of crisis, one she has never really considered. Was there truly a need to stockpile food? How did she land here? A quick glance and the list contains many of the staples the celebrity chef recommended for her "perfect pantry"; others are foreign to Martha: powdered milk and eggs, canned butter, freeze-dried food, vodka, and MREs. Canned butter? Such a thing exists? She skips over, "Desserts for the Apocalypse." A column of ads runs down the right side of the page; an attractive young woman poses, hand on hip, in camo gear, and above her a logo for Mountain House—what's that? Following the list of must-have foods is another list, this one of steps: budgeting, rotating your stockpile, buying in bulk, storing heirloom seeds. Five billion people have less than a week's worth of food at home, she learns, and when 'SHTF,' grocery stores run out of food in three days. She drops the pen, rubs her clammy hands on her jeans.

"You don't have to look far for a reason to prepare," the About Us page states. "Imminent nuclear war, environmental collapse, natural disasters, solar flares, EMPs, civil war, martial law, and terrorist attacks on our power grid all pose a threat to our fragile modern way of life. But that's why we call ourselves 'Merry Preppers'—the more you prepare, the less worried you'll be when SHTF! As you work to make yourself more resilient, remember: be discreet. Those same friends and neighbors who ridicule you for preparing will be the first of the hungry mobs to storm your house, robbing you and your family of food and essentials, and possibly killing you, in a crisis. Remember Rule Number One: What you keep on your shelf, you keep to yourself!"

Martha snaps shut the laptop, paces a few steps, then grabs her list and purse. Moments later, she combs the endless rows of the grocery store, dizzy. Is it possible, the kind of crisis that would make the delivery trucks stop coming, for long enough to cause panic? She gathers tomato paste, olive oil, wild-caught tuna, pauses, for the first time, before the wide selection of jerkies, then moves on, pauses again to stoop before big tins of powdered milk on the bottom shelf. How much is her budget? She swings by the canned goods aisle again, grabs a few more varieties of beans, does the same at the dried nuts and fruits. After all, no harm in being prepared and these are all items she uses. At the checkout, the clerk, a round-faced young woman likely in high school or college, says, "Doing a little stocking up?" Martha's pulse leaps, and she lets out a shaky laugh. "Oh, just a bit, you know, hurricane season," she says. The clerk shrugs and smiles strangely. It is May. She brushes off the bag-boy's offer of help to her car, pushes her cart at a clip, loads the trunk. The tins of gourmet sardines, anchovies, and tuna bust through the bag, and tumble across the bottom.

*

That afternoon Martha picks up a shift at Marvelous Mid-Century. As she rings up 1960s Playboys and record albums, her thoughts turn to the evening ahead, and how to avoid the crisis of a long evening alone. Her son, Steven, will arrive home at five o'clock and go for a bike ride, not get home until after dark, heat up some leftovers from the fridge, and then hole up in his room on the computer for the rest of the night. She doesn't want to end up sitting alone in the backyard again, the barren lot of the rental house still so foreign to her, crying and fighting the urge to buy a pack of cigarettes, even though she has not smoked for twenty years. She must find something to do, be among friends. Sally, who owns the vintage shop, emerges from her back office and announces she's off to pick up her son, still in high school. Thank goodness Steven is no longer in school, and Martha doesn't even mind he didn't go to college but found a simple job as a bike mechanic at a mom-and-pop; his autism steers him toward the repetitive and tactile. He'll never live on his own, of course, and

Martha is lucky to have a lifelong friend in Sally, who is luckier still to have alimony and child support, enough to fund her next chapter as entrepreneur. Otherwise, Sally would be in Martha's situation— post-divorce and having to beg friends with small businesses for a part-time job after decades as a stay-at-home mom. Something they have talked about a lot, over wine at Sally's. Three years out and Sally is now comfortable in her post-divorce skin, whereas all Martha feels is unmoored.

"Is there anything going on tonight?" Martha asks. "Any art openings, jazz shows, that type of thing? If I stay home one more night I'm going to fall apart."

"Don't do that," Sally says, fumbling with her large purse, laptop, and bank deposit. "I'm supposed to meet Jason to hear a Latin band. Why don't you come?"

"Third wheel. Great."

"With us? Don't be silly. Just come." Sally's voice bounces off the back hallway, and the alarm beeps as she exits.

Customers drift in and out as closing time approaches, and Martha takes solace in the pleasant, if perfunctory exchanges, the bands of her high school days playing on the Zenith, the finds people bring to the counter: a macramé wall hanging, a Members Only jacket, a breadbox. But as soon as she locks up and climbs into her car, loneliness enshrouds her. She takes a side road, avoids going through her old neighborhood. Up until a few months ago, she was living in the house she and Warren , her ex-husband, owned for twenty years, a two-story five-bedroom with wide porches and a pool. She stayed in the house until the divorce went through and it finally sold. At least she found a rental in a decent, middle class neighborhood, behind a Publix. The mid-century concrete block ranch badly needs remodeling. She hates how quickly the dust collects on the hardwood floors, and no matter how often she scrubs the countertops, the kitchen never feels clean. She heats up leftover pasta, hastily eats alone. Next door someone bangs the screen. Then yelling, a thud, and someone drags a trash can to the curb. She knows no one on this street. The house diagonal from hers is shuttered, the car covered—snowbirds, her guess—and the house on the corner is another rental, four cars in the driveway, its inhabitants often blasting loud music.

What happened to her home? Her life? Because she doesn't feel like she has one; her husband tore that from underneath them both. Only he has his new townhouse with his mistress—now girlfriend—and she's here, left to piece together what's left. What is left, at forty-nine? Her breathing shakes a little as she applies her makeup , and she pauses to clutch the counter and steady herself. What's going to happen to her—no resume, no skills, and the alimony barely covers expenses. And when that runs out in a few years? Warren blew so much money; they have practically nothing saved for retirement. Eighty years old, will she still be working in a vintage shop? Grief and depression have shattered all her illusions that the world is safe, and able to provide happiness. How to get that back, and will she ever feel anything other than beaten up, weakened by distrust? She turns out the lights and flees to her car as if pursued by ghouls.

Martha meets Sally in Winter Park, at a jazz club located inside a converted warehouse. Sally orders a cabernet; Martha, as much as she wants a drink, orders a sparkling water instead. The two sit at a cocktail table, the sparkling water fizzy and bland. Martha says, "How long did this last for you? I mean, what else do I do? Every day I can barely function."

"You're doing the best you can. Go easy on yourself." Sally sips her wine, gives a little wave to Jason, whom she's been seeing for seven months. Jason, tall and lean, bends to check sound equipment on the stage; he's a musician, helps run the place. "What else should you be doing? Just get out, meet people. Like tonight."

"Sure. As long as they know I'm in no shape for dating."

"Of course not. That's the last thing you need. Just live your life. What about taking up some new interest or hobby?" The band trickles out, settles into instruments. Jason strolls over, clasps Sally's hand and sits. He's some kind of engineer by day. Sally met him after a literary event. "Life falls into place like love—when you're not looking for it."

"A hobby—I can't even think of what. That's just it, I can't think. Everything is a fog." Martha munches goldfish crackers, dismisses the thought of how they're loaded with salt and fake dye.

"Look, for me it's taken three years to get here." Sally pats Jason's forearm—rather hairy, Martha thinks. Her husband had beautiful forearms and hands. Like a Michelangelo. "What did I do? Started the shop, that certainly kept me busy. Exercised. All that-be-kind-to-yourself stuff."

"Nothing feels like my life. Even cooking. I've lost my passion."

"Hey look," Jason says, and leans in. "At least you're not in Venezuela right now. You know what one of the guys up there just told me—the drummer? That back in his parents' neighborhood gangs have taken over the streets, running black markets. That they're charging crazy prices for a sliver of soap or deodorant, and people are so desperate they're lining up to pay for these guys to cut them a tiny wedge off a cake. Imagine that, huh?" The lights dim; Martha's stomach sinks. "Not to make light what you're going through—I've been there, myself—but hell! Could be worse. You're gonna be okay."

The band starts, the stage awash in a bluish tinge. The drummer wears a big smile, body rocking as he plays, trance-like. On either side the seats brim with silver and grey heads, wrinkled necks, spotted hands. Lately she finds herself humbled and in awe at those who have lived so long—even for those comfortable enough to afford the cover charge and a bottle of wine, like the elderly couple to her right, the man slightly hunched and wheezy, the woman stout and fidgeting, both neatly attired in blazers and dress shoes. What have they endured? Another three, even four decades, fraught with more losses and heartbreak—how will she make it? The music cocoons her, a temporary shelter. Maybe that's enough sometimes, just to get you from place to place.

Driving home she thinks of what Jason said, about the crisis in Venezuela. Not long ago, wasn't that the most prosperous South American country? If that kind of collapse happens here (and who is to say it couldn't—look at how her own life fell apart, out of nowhere), shouldn't she also have toiletries and basic first aid items on hand? At the intersection nearest her house, the 24-hour Walgreen's stands aglow, a temple of simple, yet vital, necessities. It's nearly eleven, but she parks, hurries in. Where to begin? She squints. Soap and deodorant are a no-brainer, after the story from earlier; she grabs a three-pack of each. Bottles of ibuprofen and aspirin, razors, toothpaste and floss, baby powder, contact lens solution. First aid: assortment packs of Band-aids, creams, ointments, gauze, hydrogen peroxide and rubbing alcohol, iodine, witch hazel. What about lice treatment? Hand sanitizer, suntan lotion, bug spray, aloe, Imodium, tea tree oil, disinfectant wipes. Q-tips, cotton balls, nail files, face cream, cough drops. The heavier the basket grows, the more its contents pull her along, but slowly—she needs to take in the aisles, be sure she's not missing something. Only when the items are falling from the top does she plunk her selections before the clerk. The customer before her, a gritty-looking man in stained jeans, warily eyes her basket as he grabs his pack of cigarettes and Dr. Pepper.

It's past midnight when she bursts in the front door, sets down the two bags like barbells. Steven's door is open, computer casting him in silhouette. She calls out hello. He ambles out, crusty pasta bowl in hand, stops. "What's all that?" he asks, bloodshot eyes narrowing. "Oh, just some bathroom stuff," she says, shuffling past. She kneels and makes room below the sink for the peroxide and other tall bottles. Back in his room, Steven says, "I've found the most insane electric bicycles on YouTube, you'll never believe it." Martha listens to him describe the details as she shoves her purchases in the drawers and medicine chest, says how interesting that is, how neat that he came across such bikes. Another twentysomething son might say, "You went to Walgreen's at midnight?" But she knows never to expect that from Steven. His mind is a monorail, gliding on the same well-worn path.

Finished, something in her feels quelled—not quite like she smoked a cigarette, but almost. She peels off her clothes, elated, and flops on the bed. She's not going to be screwed over for a sliver of soap, not after everything she's been through—she's got her own, and plenty, thank you very much! Just let them try.

*

Martha decides to consult MerryPreppers.com again, about the pantry essentials. But she ends up reading about water. Contamination is evidently a huge problem in any crisis, and poor sanitation quickly leads to the spread of disease—she knows this, but how has she taken such a vital necessity for granted all her life? In a short-term crisis, water service may be restored in days or weeks, but a larger event such as a solar flare or EMP could disrupt power and water treatment plants for years. MerryPreppers recommends several water filters offered by one of their sponsors. Martha follows the link to Amazon, selects a water filter widely used in developing countries. The filter can supposedly kill 99% of bacteria and pathogens and supply a household with clean water for up to three years. Other customers also bought purification tablets; she adds these too. Is that sufficient? She's not sure, but this is all her budget will allow, for now. Her total comes to just under one hundred dollars. Before she clicks "pay," she notes the row of suggested items and clicks across. Inflatable water "bricks," reverse-osmosis pitchers that remove radioactivity, IOSAT tablets—what is all this, and who is buying these things? Does she really think she is ever going to use this filter? Maybe not, but she likes knowing that she'll be prepared. She writes on her list, in what she has learned is order of necessity: "water, food, shelter, protection." Then crosses out "protection" and writes "guns."

All throughout the week, in between ringing up vintage TV Guides and Polaroid cameras, she visits different prepper sites, creates lists of budgets and to-dos. TheMotherofAllPreppers.com provides lots of handy PDFs and checklists, which she later prints out at home.

OrganicSurvivalist.com shows a comprehensive chart of tried-and-true emergency heirloom seed vaults; maybe she'll get into gardening, after all. PrepperJane.com advocates to female preppers that "just because SHTF, there's no reason to have to go without makeup" and offers an e-book on DIY recipes for face and body products when you buy from her essential oil line. Some of the more male-authored sites she visits, too—lots of ex-military and special ops persons, eager and willing to share expertise, with a focus on defense, guns and ammo, and "bugging out" upon wilderness terrain. At SurviveCollapse.com, she follows debates about which freeze-dried food companies offer the best quality and which to avoid, whether she ought to buy ready-to-eat meals. Her wish list on Amazon grows.

One day when she's home the mailman's radio squawks as he climbs the porch steps. A moment later, the bell trills. She leaps up, swings open the door. "Here you go," he says gaily and thrusts forward a package first, then her mail. "Oh," she says, surprised—it's for Steven, a bicycle battery he's long awaited from China. The mailman pushes up his shades, turns away.

"Wait," she says. "I'll be receiving more packages soon. If you could just stick them here"—she jerks the porch chair forward, gestures to the space behind, shaded by a potted plant—"I would really appreciate it."

"Hide them, you mean?" He gives a curt nod. "Sure thing. Thieves swiping packages off porches is rampant, unfortunately." Sweat masks his face, the bottom of his thick moustache dark with damp.

*

"Have you ever taken one of those women's self-defense classes?" Martha asks Sally. Heat blurs the vacant parking lot of Marvelous Mid-Century. Sally is changing out a mannequin for June, from sharp-cornered mod dress to lacy wedding gown, while Martha reorganizes a jewelry case. "You know, the free ones the police department gives?"

"No." Sally wrestles with the mannequin's arm, which refuses to snap into place. "Why?"

"Why not?" Martha fiddles with the antique silver bands, spreading out the variety of gemstones. Sally's written a little sign: PERFECT ENGAGEMENT RINGS—20% off! "Didn't finding yourself suddenly alone make you feel unsafe—vulnerable?" She bumps a metal tree and the chandelier earrings shake. "Maybe I'm just feeling so raw that I'm paranoid."

"Has working here helped at all? I hope," Sally adds with a chuckle. "What about something fun, like going on a trip? Or an art class, or a writing group. You know, express your feelings."

"I'm too Mary Poppins for that."

"I know, I'm being a smartass." The alabaster arm snaps into place.

"In the winter it's dark out when we close up. The craft beer place next door got robbed." Martha props the sign beside the rings—sapphires sell the best—and locks the case. "There's a class this Saturday at noon."

"Only if we can go to lunch afterward." Sally flits to the hat display, and Martha resumes her place behind the register. A woman their age pulls up and gets out of her Mercedes, slings her yoga mat onto her mole-speckled but well-toned back. She walks erect, purposefully into the studio next door, reusable water bottle in hand. A pang of longing erupts in Martha's sternum, a churning mix of jealousy and mourning. The 3:30 Happy Flow—that used to be the class she attended. Jaw set, she blinks back hot tears. David Bowie sings from the speakers. Beneath the plaza sign the sun's rays glare off a vagrant man's shopping cart.

*

Martha doesn't tell Sally, but she attends a foraging class in Jay Blanchard Park in the early morning before they're to meet at the Winter Park Police Department. The teacher is somewhat of a celebrity in the small world of 'wild edibles' and goes by the name Wildman Pete. When Martha shows up she finds herself with a half-dozen others who gather around Wildman Pete, a slack-muscled old hippy who speaks so many details so quickly she scrambles to keep up. Threads hang from his paisley shirt sleeves and he uses a walking stick—Pete's wild days, if he ever had any, clearly behind him. Most annoying to Martha is the perky single woman in a floppy sunhat who keeps interrupting Wildman Pete, taking notes, and sidling up to Martha to make inappropriate remarks, as if they were best friends. Wildman Pete leads them along the riverbank.

"That there white flowering plant is the water hemlock," he says, pointing with a Bowie knife, its handle made of something resembling bone or horn. "We're not going to get one step nearer." Ingesting any water hemlock, he tells them, results in a sure death— no antidote—with convulsions so violent they can break bones within forty-five minutes. There were even cases of people who whittled flutes by mistake from water hemlock, and died right after playing their first song.

The woman nudges Martha, and says, so close Martha can smell her cinnamon gum, "Comes in handy, you decide to get rid of your ex-husband after all, once civilization comes down, right? Who's gonna know?" She laughs hard, to herself; Martha politely titters. For the rest of the class the woman interrupts and nags Wildman Pete to talk more about mushrooms and hallucinogens that can be used for shamanistic journeys and "inner work."

The story makes a good one over lunch, although Martha is careful to tell Sally she went to a "gardening class," not foraging, and avoid raising suspicion. They're sitting outside on Park Avenue, thinly-sliced cucumbers floating atop their iced water. The hour-long self-defense class was basic and unremarkable. An officer reminded them not to use ATMs at night and, if ever apprehended, to scream and kick just hard enough to run away. His partner came around with a mat; they struck with their palms and screamed "No!" from their guts. At the end the cops handed out keychain whistles with flashlights and pens which advertised the police department.

"That woman was a lunatic," Martha says, and sips some water. A chilled sauvignon blanc sweats before Sally. "But still, I want to take more of these classes."

"How about salsa?" Sally sits forward, fingertips together. "Get those endorphins going? Maybe—maybe!—meet someone?"

"I really liked that hitting we did, you know?" Martha mimics the palm-thrust they learned mid-air. "And I never thought of myself as angry before? Did you feel that?"

"Somewhat," Sally says. Salads arrive. "I felt more powerful than I expected."

"Exactly." Martha smiles, picks up her knife and fork.

"Are you seriously thinking of trying martial arts?"

"I need the exercise." Across from them the waiter kneels and sets down a bowl of water before a panting, black-and-white Great Dane. "And, I'm thinking about getting a dog."

"A dog—but you hate dogs! You've always been a cat person."

The couple one table over falls silent. Martha raises her eyebrows and stifles a laugh. Sally's hand flies to her mouth, and she flushes red up to her blonde roots. "I mean, what would you do about your cats?" Sally says, more softly this time.

"Oh, I don't know. I'm just thinking how this year is all about embracing change, taking back my life. Not being a victim of circumstance." She laces her fingers together; the phantom circle where her rings used to reside feels too naked, like a missing limb. The Great Dane rises, drinks sloppily from the bowl, drenching the sidewalk. Martha says, "I'd have to walk a dog, which would also get me in shape and out of the house—there you go, I might meet someone."

"I've never heard you so obsessed about getting into shape." Sally's forehead wrinkles as she takes another bite of salad.

"Getting in shape is number one." Martha's tone is emphatic; she stops herself just in time. Remember the First Rule, she thinks, and changes the subject. When Sally leaves to use the restroom Martha digs out the plastic whistle, fixes it to her keychain.

At home, boxes are piled up inside the front door. Steven is off from work, holed up in his room but appears, squinting, to intercept her. "These are addressed to you but I think some of these are a mistake," he says, picks one up and frowns as he reads aloud. "Solar Cookers International? What's that?"

She grabs the box. "Nope, I ordered some things."

"Some weird things. What's a solar cooker?"

"Never mind, it's just some camping stuff. Hurricane prep. Hey, come with me to Home Depot in a little bit, will you? I want to get a generator, but need your help to lift it."

"Aren't generators expensive? I thought you were being careful with money."

"I am—and this is practical." The younger cat, Mr. Mike, tiger-striped, weaves between her legs and meows; the geriatric tabby, Echo, climbs down from her basket, slowly as a sloth. They trot up and hover by the food bowls; she scolds Steven for neglecting to feed them. "Dogs are a deterrent," the police officer said that morning. A quick scroll of the news reveals bank failures in Italy, power blackouts in Australia, riots in Cape Town, the water gone, dried up. Her pulse quickens. She searches "best guard dogs" and "dogs for survivalists." Mr. Mike leaps up; his tail flicks her computer screen. German Shepherds, Rottweilers, Dobermans. Is getting a dog for no other reason than protection a good idea, and does she really want to take this step? How did you know if you'd gone too far, and were in danger of becoming like the woman she'd met that morning—chattering and unhinged? Would she even know? SaavySurvivalist. com says, "Women are attacked first, then old people, children, and weak-looking men, in that order." A knot tightens in her middle. Maybe she's been going about this all wrong, and she's not as alone as she thinks. Surviving for yourself—wasn't that rather pointless? Maybe she couldn't throw lavish dinner parties anymore and go to yoga and bridge, but maybe this would toughen her up. Maybe she'll be able to help others in hard times. And her son, what about him?

"What do you think about getting a dog?" she calls to Steven. He springs to his doorway, wide-legged, and hugs his skinny arms to his chest. When he was a kid he used to love petting zoos and the class gerbils, she recalls. They can discuss the dog on the way to Home Depot, she says.

*

Martha begins karate on Tuesday nights and kickboxing on Thursday nights. Every time she lands a punch or a kick and exhales, she feels the same release as she did in the self-defense class, only now with more adrenaline—she leaves coated in sweat, and craving more. At both places she signs up for ten-class packages, buys uniforms and equipment. Several times a week the mailman or UPS driver rings the doorbell; she shoves the boxes in the hall closet and garage. A walkie-talkie set, crossbow and archery kit arrive—why not take up those next?—and freeze-dried food ordered from a company in Utah whose website features wholesome-looking blonde moms. The same company sells a food dehydrator, but she doesn't order that yet. She makes a separate list for the expensive and more complicated items: bug-out location, get-out-of-dodge vehicle, guns and body armor. When the credit card statements arrive, she trembles. To pay for the preps she will need another part-time job. She marches into the nearest REI the next day and describes her experience at the vintage store. "I haven't spent as much time in the wilderness as I'd like," she tells them. "But hopefully, I will be. With my son."

The dog Martha and Steven pick out is a smaller German Shepherd, a female, hesitant and shrewd, but friendly enough, they agree. But first there is the problem of the cats. Martha decides to try Sally, whose circle is far wider; besides, she needs to tell her about her second job. Double rows of brake lights glow red as Martha creeps along in rush hour traffic. Sally picks up on the third ring, out-of-breath. "Know anyone who's up for adopting cats?"

"Cats?" Sally says. "What are you talking about? I can't—look, Jason and I are at my house. He's just been robbed. Are you anywhere nearby?"

"Be right there." Martha whips a u-turn and barrels toward Sally's street.

Moments later, Martha hugs Sally, then Jason, the three of them gathered in Sally's living room. Sally sails over to the liquor shelf, pours bourbon and hastily passes around some ice. Jason is ashen and can't sit still; he sits, then paces. Sally remains seated but flicks her hair over her shoulder. Sally's own cat, overweight and white as an Easter bunny, rolls on the couch. "What happened?" Martha asks. Sally and Jason had just met up at his bungalow, a few streets over from Sally's, and made a quick trip to the grocery store for a few things.

"We come back, and the door is kicked in, big shoe print and everything," Jason says. "The papers are messed up on the desk, bedroom drawers all open—nothing in there but boxer briefs, good luck with that." They called the police, spoke to the neighbor, who claimed to have heard a crash just after their car left the driveway, but didn't bother to come out and see what—thought he must have heard a board falling in the garage. The medicine and kitchen cabinets were gone through, left open, vitamin bottles askew.

"Whoever broke in was a drug addict, the cops think, probably someone homeless—God knows they're around," Sally says. She smooths her hair; the ice rattles. "I feel so violated. I mean, we hadn't been gone ten minutes—what if we had been home?"

"What are you going to do now?" Martha asks. She shivers; the A/C kicks on.

"I don't know—get a dog," Sally says, and laughs. "Is that what you're up to? Finding homes for your cats?"

Jason sways, fists on hips. "Now I see how people get guns," he says, a catch in his throat.

"You're not getting a gun," Sally says quickly.

"Well, maybe I'll get a dog." He gestures toward Martha. "Nothing wrong with that. I like dogs. If I were a woman alone, I'd get one too."

Martha presses her hands between her thighs. The cat comes up and rubs her leg.

Facing the liquor cabinet, Jason splashes more bourbon into his glass, mutters something about the income inequality getting out of control. Sally leans forward. "You know what else," she says. "I heard from my sister today, out in San Francisco. You know that super wealthy family she works for, as an au pair? Well, not any-more—she says she just finished helping them pack up. They're moving to New Zealand. I asked her if she thought they had a bunker down there. She says something like that, a big off-the-grid compound. A lot of the rich people are leaving, she says. Afraid of unrest."

Martha arises, her legs watery and weak, thanks them for the drink, and to let her know if she can be of help. Only by the time she's at the stop sign does she realize she forgot to mention her new hours at the camping store.

The next morning Martha calls the breeder to confirm that she'll take the dog. Then she calls the vet and makes an appointment to euthanize Echo. Steven will be upset, but Echo is twenty and has been deaf and blind for years now. Might as well be time to say good-bye. As for Mr. Mike, she recalls reading on one of the prepper sites that the very poor in other countries eat cats, and that cat stew can be rather tasty—far tastier than dog. Her insides clench, but maybe they can try keeping Mr. Mike for now, if he lives in Steven's room. Not a very fun existence for Mr. Mike, but they'll all have to make sacrifices. Better to decide now who to be, she thinks, and mercy is easier when you have a full stomach.

*

A few weeks later, Martha is as toned and buff as the women she once envied who emerged from yoga. At REI she so casually inserts the Rule of Three into her pitches—"three hours without shelter, three days without water, three weeks without food"—that her sales jump to the front of the team; the manager bumps her up to full-time, and Martha gives her notice at Marvelous Mid-Century. Sometimes Sally joins her at kickboxing class and to walk Sasha, Martha's new dog. One day Sally shows up with pepper spray for each of their keychains, in breast cancer awareness pink; Martha's dangles alongside her safety class whistle. Jason is moving into Sally's house and they're installing an alarm system. In the heat the German Shepherd pants and strains and takes huge shits. Martha cringes when she picks up the mounds of excrement and drops them in the little bag, but the dog-walking is also keeping her in shape. Her days are full and she has never felt so healthy. She can feel the ground beneath her feet again, even if what lies ahead doesn't resemble at all her former life.

By the height of summer, tropical storms are churning in the Atlantic, one angry white pinwheel after another. Sooner or later a depression will turn into a hurricane. MerryPreppers mentions having a "Merry Survival At-Home Weekend" where you hunker down and try out your preps, troubleshooting whatever may arise to avoid snags in an actual emergency. She has no plans for the 4th of July and Steven is going to the Keys with his father. The store has been slow; she gives away the rest of her shifts. On that Saturday she makes sure the propane tanks are full. She's bought a few more things with her employee discount: a tent, sleeping bag and pillow, a camp shower. Just me and the raccoons in the backyard, she laughs to herself. Reading online she learns how to turn off the main breaker for the house electricity so she can hook up the generator, unused until now. Before Steven leaves she gets him to help her haul the generator outside, under the deck in case of rain; alone she manages to hook up the proper plugs and cords. In a huff the machine chugs to life: the fridge hums, the ceiling fans spin. Steven will be so proud, she thinks. Just in time, too—dark clouds rolling in and breeze kicking up. She hurries inside to reward herself, opens a bag of freeze-dried spaghetti and meatballs, then brings a treat to the dog who lies beneath the couch. Sasha opens one eye as she approaches, yawns wide, and takes the treat.

Martha turns off the A/C to not strain the generator, and the house quickly grows warm. Somewhere in the neighborhood, a couple of firecrackers sound off early. "Survival scenarios often involve more boredom than the average person expects," according to SavvyPreppers—or did she read that on PrepperJane? She lies down, sleepy, and to her surprise Mr. Mike trots out of the bedroom, onto the back of the couch, and curls up at her feet. She'll never be hungry, or have to drink dirty water. She'll never be without shelter.

But in three minutes, she'll be without air. At the end of the weekend Steven will come home and find Martha's body, her lips cherry red. By her feet will lie the cat and dog, stiffened and silent. "Carbon monoxide poisoning," the cop will say, pat Steven on the back as they wheel out his mother under a dark sheet. "Common mistake with generators—run them someplace like that deck, and you get a wind that blows a certain way, the fumes find their way into the vents and crawlspace pretty fast, and you're dead." Sally and Jason will sit on the porch, and weep. Carefully tucked behind the potted plant will be a brown package, and within the bouquet of mail an invitation to NRA membership.

For now, Martha is falling asleep. That spaghetti and meatballs was salty and is making her feel constipated—queasy, too. She frowns and yawns. All these water purification tablets and the antibiotic travel kit—before the world goes to hell, maybe she'll take Steven on a trip to Thailand. Learn to run your life, or your life runs you. She closes her eyes. Sapphire water, sugar sand, towering isles of limestone rock.

PERFECT CONDITIONS

Mid-afternoon, a red cab pulled into the flooding lot of the Autotica repair shop. The shop's owner hung back and took in the passenger who stepped out: the skinny jeans and easy way the young man swung his bag onto his shoulder, despite the shocking softness in the once-hardened arms sticking out from his t-shirt. The visitor grimaced against the streaming rain, jagged black hair plastered against his pale face, one that Jack hadn't seen for some time and strained to recognize—his son. Jack felt as if he were floating on his surfboard in the thin gray of dawn, the face of a sudden and monstrous Pacific swell rushing towards him. His ex-wife, Linda, had told him that Sebastian didn't work in Japan, that he lived as a sort of kept man, and well-to-do Japanese women paid for his expenses in exchange for sex with an attractive gaijin whom they could show off as a boyfriend.

"He calls it a 'lifestyle,'" she said, her voice wavering.

Now Sebastian approached and raised one hand overhead, and Jack stood there for a moment before realizing that his son was initiating a high-five. The two Tico mechanics—one with the barest trail of fuzz on his upper lip, the other a fresh-faced new hire—looked up from the Mitsubishi they were working on, and exchanged a bemused sidelong glance. Jack released a sheepish laugh, curled an arm around Sebastian, and drew him into a hug. "You eat anything besides sushi these days?" Jack asked. He hoped some light banter might mask any alarm. "How's your skinny ass gonna handle a board?"

"Cut it out, course I can," Sebastian said with a smirk. "Funky place you've got." He swung down his bag and, with two silver-ringed fingers, traced the Mitsubishi's handlebars. The slighter young mechanic scooted on his back beneath the jet-ski while the other instructed sharply from above, foot resting upon the dented bumper of a mud-splattered Land Rover. Sand-dusted surfboards of different heights and shapes guarded the door to Jack's cluttered office. The boards tilted into one another like dominoes.

"Not much to Jacó," Jack said. He climbed to the second-floor apartment above, steps slippery and squeaking as Sebastian trailed, kicking off his flip-flops atop a pile of cracked and soggy booties before entering. "Surfers and some bars, a ratty casino," Jack added. They ducked inside. "Rains like this all afternoon in the green season. But if we rise and shine early, I promise we'll catch some gorgeous surf. I've been counting down the days, man. Can't wait to catch up with you." He squeezed Sebastian's shoulder; the bone wedged into his palm like the edge of a seashell. Sebastian was gaunt, even sickly looking—too much indoor living: take-out, video games, weed? Or a party lifestyle gone too far? Jack hastily reached for a towel and handed it over. Sebastian carefully dried off, the wet hair plastered to his face making him look boyish. His plain undershirt, still damp, shifted to reveal a wide tattoo across his caved-in chest, Jack couldn't make out what. A tightness sprang to Jack's throat as he took back the towel and patted himself dry. "You hungry? Want something to eat?"

"Not really. Still got a funky benzo headache from the plane. Got any green tea?"

"Tea—no. Coffee?"

"Forget it. I'm fine."

"Quite the rock star get-up you have going on. Aren't you going to be twenty-six next month?"

"Twenty-seven."

Cheeks flushed, Jack rattled around the DVD player, popped in a surfing movie. Sebastian settled on one side of the couch. Jack sat on the other and began rolling a joint. "So, Japan?" Jack asked. "Your mom tells me you've got quite a life there."

"You should visit sometime. The women, they're very—dutiful." The dot of a birthmark just grazed his upper lip as he grinned. He hadn't removed his shoes—pointy-toed black ankle boots, now drenched. He extended his legs in a V, the wet soles leaving dark circles on the worn carpet like pools of blood.

Onscreen, the surfer and jet-ski parted, the wall of water upon them. "Tokyo's one of the most expensive cities in the world, right?" Jack asked. "How do you earn a living?"

"I don't."

"Your mother mentioned some kind of arrangement."

"Japan has a little bit of a problem with eligible bachelors. Some of the career ladies are more interested in sex than the rest of their peers."

"Aren't there other ways of making the rent?"

"Sure. But I'm hardly the only one doing this." Sebastian leaned forward. "Is that you?" He nodded at the screen.

"I'm on the jet-ski," Jack said quickly, gesturing to the right corner. "Big surf like that beat me up too bad. That's where I make my money now, mainly. Dudes come down here from all over, and I tow them in." He raised an elbow overhead, stretched his shoulder, which popped and creaked as if on cue.

The muted jet-skis charged across the screen, and the ocean swelled. Sebastian's mother had called up several weeks back, sobbing and nearly hysterical over the fact that she barely heard from their only child anymore. Jack was worried, too. On the rare occasion he would catch Sebastian on Skype and press for a visit, his son either grew quiet or abruptly changed the subject. "What if you pay for the airfare?" Linda had said. "Is he really going to refuse?" Her voice rang with a desperation that echoed long after they spoke, distracting Jack from his shop duties. He had thought his anxiety would be relieved once he contacted Sebastian and offered to buy the ticket. After a day or so, Sebastian returned his call and said yes, he'd like to come and accepted the ticket offer, although he hastily assured Jack that he had his own money. So why take up Jack's invitation to visit now, after distancing himself for so long—and why was he keeping so distant? Had Jack done something wrong that Sebastian resented? Or was Sebastian living a life he saw as bohemian and glamorous— an example Jack had set during his marriage? "Traveling feeds the soul," he'd always said, partly as a way of masking what he hated about his job: consulting for international hotels. Overseas adventure was a virtue lacking in most Americans, and he felt sure he'd been a good role model for his only son.

"There are a lot of ways to live," Jack said. He sparked the joint. "It takes a while to figure these things out."

Sebastian slumped back, hugged himself. "I sure never pictured you in the Third World, surfing and running a mechanic shop."

Jack offered the joint; Sebastian waved it off. The towering break devoured the surfer in its white, foaming belly, and the darting speck that was Jack onscreen circled in the churning stew to pull out its victim.

*

While Sebastian napped, Jack slipped downstairs to close up. He counted the tools to make sure none had gone missing, and checked the engine work on the Mitsubishi. The last time he'd seen Sebastian was five years ago, right before he had quit consulting and left the States. Sebastian had been sturdy then, not one bit the waif who washed up today. And his clothes, those boots—didn't he have the sense to bring shorts and practical shoes to Costa Rica? The last time they'd gone surfing back home at New Smyrna, Jack had thought about how lucky Sebastian was at twenty-one: good-looking and able to build easy rapport with people, about to surf and backpack southeast Asia, all his life ahead of him. What had made him choose this kind of lifestyle, and the people who came along with it?

Gabi, Jack's girlfriend, glided into the garage on her bike. Her poncho, neon orange, was draped tent-like over her petite frame, her face barely visible; she'd found the cast-off in a nearby ditch, left by a paving crew that had come through a couple of months prior. In addition to the auto repair shop, Jack owned a laundromat in Jacó Beach, and Gabi oversaw the facility during the day. Nights, she cooked the dishes she missed from Nicaragua and rewrote his replies to business emails in Spanish, his attempts often the subject of much laughter between them.

"Did your son arrive okay?" she asked.

"He's upstairs," Jack said. He pulled up a stool to the makeshift counter. "I was so excited for us to go surfing. But now I don't know."

She opened the grease-smudged mini-fridge and retrieved two beers, opening his first and setting the bottle in front of him. "What's wrong?"

Jack frowned, toying with the cap. He took one gulp, then another, his throat filled with sour and cold. Impossible to explain everything to Gabi, a couple of years younger than Sebastian. She had cared for five younger siblings while her parents worked and had never once dropped out of school—she would say this proudly, chin lifted. After she and her brother had both graduated they headed south, determined to find better jobs in Costa Rica. A simple life was all Gabi knew, nothing of the world but her village in Nicaragua and the Pacific side of Costa Rica, and what Jack had been longing for. He hadn't even bothered to install cable or a satellite in the apartment; he just surfed and breathed in the salt air when he could, then went back to running the mechanics, the grime and fumes, diesel and heat. Searching for small, clean sets breaking just offshore in the first moments of morning, from Jacó to Playa Hermosa and further south, remained his source of joy and solace. The smaller sets would be perfect to ride with Sebastian, might even bring him back from whatever spiral he'd been sucked down, if he was indeed running with a bad crowd.

Bottle empty, Jack yanked down the chain-link gate at the garage entrance. The night bugs and frogs croaked, more a racket than a concert, the padlock scratched and heavy. Footsteps rocked the stairwell; it shimmied, and Sebastian appeared, holding up Gabi's laptop with one hand like a server breezing by with drinks. Gabi shot Jack a sharp, panicked glance. "Hey," she cried. "Careful with that!"

"Easy there," Jack said. "That's got all the surfing footage Gabi's shot this year."

"Gabi?" Sebastian set down the laptop beside the beers.

"Mucho gusto," Gabi said. She extended her hand. Sebastian returned a limp shake, but nodded affably. He'd changed into a well-worn pair of boardshorts that Jack remembered him wearing back in Florida. Jack had given him the shorts for a birthday—his eighteenth—plus thrown him a huge luau. They'd even roasted a pig in the yard. He wondered if Sebastian remembered that.

"I'll take one of those," Sebastian said. "If you don't mind." He leaned on his elbows across the counter and smiled. Gabi fetched another beer, opened it, and set it in front of Sebastian.

"Gabi and I have been together for a couple of years now," Jack said. "We've been talking about getting married next year."

"You mean I've been talking about it," Gabi said, and flicked Jack's arm. They laughed.

Sebastian lifted the bottle, and eyes narrowed at the screen. "You didn't tell me Jacó has a big party scene. How's the vibe? Any good music?"

"Oh, Jacó's got her fair share of whore bars, that kind of thing," Jack said. "I don't partake, though."

"Excuse me," Gabi said. She slid over the laptop, and Sebastian straightened, eyes wide, taken aback. Swiftly, she clicked open some media files. A guitar soundtrack kicked on and a video opened to close-up footage of a surfer—crinkled, wet mop lifting behind the shoulders of a girl—cutting across a wave close to shore. "See for yourself," she said. Down her arm, slender and dark-haired, a glass-beaded bracelet jostled. "I'm not done getting the shots I need. But some companies are interested in buying my films," she said. "Rip Curl and Roxy."

"Good for you." Sebastian sipped his beer, gaze wandering off. The hulking machines of the shop loomed shadowy and still. When Gabi closed the files, Sebastian asked to check his email. Was he merely jet-lagged and short-fused, or was his coolness stemming from some deeper grudge? Jack had mentioned Gabi before, but he and Sebastian spoke so infrequently; maybe the seriousness of the relationship had come as a shock. But, his son was an adult. He would get used to it. Jack and Gabi discussed dinner—she had made tamales that morning, and if they ate at home and retired early, they could arrive at the beach by sunrise. Midway through, they switched to Spanish as though not to disturb Sebastian, who remained frozen at the computer, striking the keyboard furiously.

Soon after, all three went upstairs, and Gabi showed some newer footage to Jack, discussing possible edits over another round of beers. Sebastian disappeared, took a shower long enough to steam the hallway mirror. A heady cologne trailed him when he emerged; fire-spitting dragons snaked across the silky black of his shirt. He tugged on his boots, announced that he was going out for a bit, see the town. "You coming?" he asked Jack.

"I'm pretty beat," Jack said. "We surfing in the morning?"

"How early? Probably should have warned you: I'm more of a night person these days."

"I see that. Hitting the karaoke bars with your lady friends pretty regularly?"

"Not so much." Sebastian unplugged his phone, shoved it in his back pocket. "Computer animation. You know *Ghost in the Shell?* It's what got me hooked. I'm still learning but I'm up late most nights. Game design too."

"Animation," Jack said, taking in this turn—his beach bum son now a computer geek. "Cool."

"Too much screen time, though. I try and get out a couple nights a week." Sebastian unfolded a pair of thin, round-framed glasses, carefully put them on. Were they for show, or did he need glasses now? Hard to tell. He squinted. "I wanted to talk to you about my college fund," he said. "Since I never went. I'm serious about the game design, and my Japanese is getting better. I was wondering if I could get that money, and use it for these courses I want to take."

"Oh," Jack said. "Well, that's a plan, at least. But I won't be able to help you out, I'm afraid."

"Why not?"

"That money's gone. We gave it a few years, but once you headed off to Asia—and we didn't hear very much from you—we guessed you gave up on school for good."

Sebastian stood for a while in silence.

"Meanwhile," Jack went on, "your mother badly wanted to get her Master's, remember? So, I agreed she should use the money for that. Fair, I think, since we're the ones who earned it and put it aside."

"What's the difference if I went to school or not?" Sebastian asked. "What if I wanted to start a business instead of getting some degree? You didn't even ask me first if I'd mind. You stole it."

"Things changed. Your mother and I aren't exactly flush with cash."

"So maybe I would have wanted in on that conversation. A head's up would have been nice, and maybe I would have done things differently."

"A conversation, sure." Jack set his empty bottle down, hard. "For that to happen, we'd have to know how to actually get ahold of you. When someone answers, oh, I don't know, one out of three emails with a two-word response, it doesn't make discussion very easy. So maybe what I want to know is: why? What did we do wrong?"

"Are you kidding me?" Sebastian stood, hands on hips, slowly shaking his head. "Unbelievable, coming from you—after all the years you'd be gone for weeks, then blow back in with a bunch of stories and presents. I wonder how much money you blew, to have to rob from your own kid's future."

"Your mother and I weren't irresponsible. Some people on Wall Street were. We're lucky that we didn't put all of our eggs in one basket. And I did my best to make up for being gone—at least I tried."

"Tried. Right." Sebastian yanked his phone from its charger, shoved it in his back pocket. "I'll get the money from somewhere else." He brushed past, and left.

*

That night, Jack tossed and turned as if pinned underwater, his thoughts about Sebastian churning overhead. Had he just never known Sebastian as well as he'd thought, or had something else changed? All those years Jack had spent jetting around the world to bring in the big bucks, the six-figure salary that had allowed him to eventually quit the sixty-hour workweeks and live simply—what mark had that left on his son?

Jack remembered the phone call he'd made from Casablanca on the eve of Sebastian's fourteenth birthday. Sebastian was staying at his mother's, his first birthday following the divorce without both parents. And Jack had promised to be there. But then, through some connections, Jack was invited to a gala with the Royal Family of Morocco; all he needed to do was change his plane ticket, and the company was willing to foot the expense. Such invitations, especially in small countries, cropped up often enough, and he might have declined. Over the phone, Sebastian had insisted that Jack shouldn't miss out on meeting the Prince, the belly dancers and snake-charmers, just to fly home for his birthday. "But I don't want to miss your big day," Jack said, insistent. "That's more important to me than a bunch of hot dancers." Sebastian replied, "You're nuts then, Dad," and they'd laughed. When he hung up, he'd felt okay about changing the ticket. And the gala itself was truly spectacular. But when he returned and thrust the photos in front of Sebastian over the leftover store-bought birthday cake, Sebastian flipped through them without much comment. The boy left the room to fiddle with the thermostat before Jack even got to show him the rest—the most exciting ones, of Jack in the full Saharan garb, his blue eyes gleaming from beneath his headdress as if he'd stepped right out of *Lawrence of Arabia*.

"Too bad we got this cold snap," Jack had said. "We could have gone for a wave. Here's a funny one—check out the Jesus sandals on this dude."

Sebastian slouched in the doorway, picking absently at his elbow—scabbed, Jack guessed, from a skateboard fall. "We had perfect conditions for the last couple of weeks," the boy said. "Right up through my birthday."

Jack set the pictures aside. "Well, next year I probably won't be in the North Africa. How about that learner's permit?"

"That's not this year, Dad."

Sebastian wandered off, and minutes later the sound of his skateboard clacking down the sidewalk quickly grew faint. His silence told Jack everything. Even if the kid had thought getting invited to a royal gala was cool (maybe the result of too many movies), his father had chosen meeting the prince of a country that meant nothing to him, a place full of tents and sand, over his birthday. And the following year, Jack missed Sebastian's birthday again, this time due to a cancelled flight out of Hong Kong. He had cursed the cancelled flight, but ended up meeting his next girlfriend during that extended stay. Had he told himself he was providing and setting a bold, independent example, when he had been chasing his own happiness all the time? Even if he hadn't, maybe his noble intentions didn't matter—his simply not being there read as abandonment to his adolescent son.

When Sebastian was born, Jack had insisted on naming the boy after the inlet where he had first discovered his own passion for surfing in his youth. And for years, riding waves had been the bond between them, no matter how many days a year he spent out of the country; occasionally they would even arise together in the predawn light to go surfing before he had to fly out. He thought of when he first helped Sebastian stand up on his board on that same beach, the lightness of the boy at three years old as he carried him on his shoulders, the waves bursting against his arms and chest, the heat of the sun on his face. How he loved his son still, but somehow that person had been swept away, replaced by a stranger—a gaijin.

*

A lone rooster crowed, and Jack awoke in the darkness. He and Gabi softly padded around; she gathered the camera gear, the boards and towels. Sebastian, tucked in the fetal position beneath a sheet on the couch, didn't stir, the rise and fall of his breath measured and shallow. Jack hovered, wondering if he should wake him or not. Sebastian was so pale—paler than he'd ever seen. Could that be from living in Tokyo, the pollution and cramped space? Surely that kind of living wasn't healthy.

"I'll leave him a note," Jack whispered to Gabi. He scratched his mobile number and "Este Rios," a good sunrise break, on the back of Sebastian's baggage claim stub and propped it atop his son's charging cell phone.

Stepping onto the landing, he stumbled. Sebastian's boots jutted at the base of the sandal tower. Swearing, he tidied the stack. From the bottom of the stairs Gabi stifled a laugh. He drove the winding road south of Jacó to Playa Hermosa, Gabi in the passenger seat of the Montero SUV and the windows rolled down. Neither of them said anything. The chortles of the birds and buzzes of the insects rushed in as the truck sped past the darkened rainforest, the air humid as the breath of an ancient beast. The warm air collided with the roar of the ocean. At Este Rios he pulled down the sandy lane, parked, and surveyed the break while eating a protein bar, the faint sunlight casting the tide in an otherworldly glow. As he tugged out his board his shoulder screamed in pain, so he popped a Celebrex; time to pretend the agony away. "I'll surf until I'm too broken to get up," he'd always told his friends. All too soon, he thought, that day was coming.

After an hour in the water, Jack paddled in for a rest, eager for a breakfast of gallo pinto at the beach shack he and Gabi frequented. A hundred meters off, Gabi stooped behind her tripod in the higher, dry sand, where she was filming some young Tico surfers riding the bigger break. Jack motioned for her to meet him at the truck. As he approached the Montero he was surprised to see Sebastian in the passenger seat—was he sleeping? He must have taken a taxi, then chased down Gabi for the key.

"Why didn't you grab a board and come out?" Jack called. "Nice clean sets. Perfect as you can get."

"Jet-lag." Sebastian stretched but stayed in his seat. "Or did you forget?"

Jack toweled off in silence. After a moment, he said, "Well, I stuck a board in back, just in case you change your mind. Should be just the right size." On the break a local kid carved and wiped out, climbed back atop his board. Gabi was heading for the truck. Jack waved but she didn't respond, just strode toward them at a measured pace.

"How'd you get her to go out with your geezer ass?" Sebastian asked, eyeing Gabi in the side-mirror. "Pick her up on some corner? You don't frequent bars for that kind of thing, after all."

Jack threw his towel in the back. "Not every poor girl you meet down here is a whore. Never mind this happens to be the easiest relationship of my life."

"Easiest?"

"Peaceful." Jack squinted, stuck his head in the open window. The grittiness of recent cigarette smoke—Sebastian's—and sunscreen stung his nostrils. "Plus what exactly are you doing in Japan, huh? We better not be talking illegal—"

"What if I told you I've been shooting porn, huh? Porn's not illegal."

"Well, are you?"

"I have a couple of wealthy sponsors who like to pamper me, and party. That's all. It's not illegal."

"But why do that—be some slave to their whims?"

"We're all slaves to money, if you haven't noticed." Sebastian's gaze narrowed once again on the mirror. "Doesn't change the fact that piece of ass could be my sister."

Heat prickled Jack's face and neck. "Whatever problem you have with me, leave her out of it, okay?"

"I went out last night," Sebastian said quietly, head against the rest. "They'll do anything to get with a gringo. You're stupid if you don't see that."

Gabi opened the trunk. A plastic bag rustled; she nestled the tripod in the back. "Ready to eat?" she asked, and caught Jack's eye. She bowed her head but not before Jack saw her fury. "I took a lot of good movies," she said absently, fussing over the equipment. Sebastian and Gabi made eye contact in the rearview mirror, but Gabi averted her gaze.

Sebastian reclined the passenger seat, adjusted his sunglasses. "Have a good time."

Jack slammed shut the trunk so hard that the Montero quaked. He grabbed Gabi's hand and together they headed for the breakfast shack. A mutt belonging to the Tico surfers jogged up and, even though Jack recognized the creature, he shooed her away. Gabi let go of his hand and crossed her arms. Jack asked her what was wrong. "Your son," she said, and pressed her lips together harder. She took a few more steps before she spun around to face him. "I don't know how you say it in English."

"What is it in Spanish?" he asked. She told him. He might have suspected as much. After Sebastian had arrived in a cab at the beach that morning, he found Gabi and asked her to let him in the truck. She went back with him to change out a camera lens. Sebastian surprised her from behind, grabbed her and tried to kiss her, and felt up her breast. "Estupido," she said now, rolling her eyes, now shiny with tears. "I was so upset, I never got the shot I was going for."

Jack took Gabi's hand, rubbed it. "Thanks for telling me," he said. "I'm so sorry. This behavior—he never used to act like this."

Before he knew what was happening, he was charging back to the truck. He wrenched the door open so hard that Sebastian, startled, half-spilled out. Jack said, "Get up."

"What the hell?"

Jack reached over and ripped the sunglasses off his son's face. "Don't play stupid. You assaulted Gabi."

"You believe her?" Sebastian grabbed the door, pulled himself up. "That's it, you're just going to accuse me?"

Jack shoved his son in the chest, hard. Sebastian staggered, falling into the sand. "Don't bullshit me," Jack said. "Apologize."

"Jesus, all right! I'm sorry for being too friendly."

"And you're going to apologize to Gabi, when she comes back, and mean it. You don't change your behavior while you're here, and come clean about what your issues are with me, and we're going to have a serious problem. Got that?" Jack chucked Sebastian's sunglasses—expensive, he noted—at Sebastian's feet.

When he got back to the shack, Gabi had already ordered for them. A group of gringo surfers waited in line, all of them Sebastian's age, the one closest to Jack a bundle of smells: sun lotion, latex, salt, Tiger Balm, sweat. Blonde dreadlocks gathered at the nape of his neck, cascaded down his backbone. He was of average height but knotted with muscles. Someone told a joke, and they all laughed; the fuzzy spikes shook. Two of his buddies had matching tattoos on their calves—the real kind, from the South Pacific. Grease sizzled; his stomach rolled. Jack fished a fly out of his smoothie, told Gabi what had happened at the Montero. "I could have punched him, came this close," he mumbled.

Gabi shrugged, stirred her smoothie. "Sometimes this happens when you haven't seen each other for a long time. It happens with me and my older brother when I go back to Nicaragua. After a few days, everyone starts fighting."

"I'm not sure this is the same thing," Jack said. He stretched out his legs, relieving the cramps in his knees. "He was such a good kid, you wouldn't believe it. Maybe I should have gone to visit him sooner, overseas. Just shown up, instead of letting him run away from whatever's bugging him"

"His behavior, I don't understand," Gabi said. "You are not retired, you know? You bought the shop, repaired it. Making a new life in another country is difficult. You have to become a new person. Remember how bad your Spanish was when we met?" She squeezed his hand. A new dark blemish bloomed on his skin: another age spot. "My mother, I send money to her, you know? All those bracelets I make and sell, that's why I do that. I'm an adult. I don't expect her help." Gabi sat erect, her eyebrows, dark and thick, knit together.

"He doesn't give a shit. The way he's talking about Japan and women—I just don't get it. That porn comment—God, I hope he was just being crass. Did I mess him up this badly? His mother, she didn't abandon him."

Gabi stared at the swells. "Maybe he does resent you for some things. But I think he has different problems now."

Far off, Sebastian waded to the Pacific's edge. He stood there, alone, arms dangling, bent down and splashed, but went no farther. How much of the truth had Sebastian told? Maybe he'd gotten involved in something much darker and more sinister than paying his bills as an escort. The shorts, faded, hung limply upon his narrow waist.

*

Sebastian remained sullen for the rest of the morning and curtly apologized to Gabi. The three rode back in stony silence. Sebastian bolted upstairs and Gabi rode off to the laundromat, while Jack busied himself in the shop. The green season sometimes meant good business, with people bringing in repairs they'd otherwise been putting off. Jack was tuning up a jet-ski that belonged to another gringo surfer in Jacó when an expat acquaintance of his, resettled outside San José, stopped by with his girlfriend, a young American woman a few years older than Gabi. They were on their way to Manuel Antonio for the weekend. Jack led them upstairs to show them Gabi's surf footage and meet Sebastian. When Jack opened the door Sebastian was sprawled on the couch, sleeping, sheet askew. It was almost three in the afternoon. Jack ushered the friends back downstairs, fuming.

Animation—shouldn't that have come as a relief, that his son was doing something productive, and creative at that? So why didn't Jack feel relieved? Maybe because he sensed Sebastian wasn't being entirely sincere, and resented Jack no matter what. Had he just come to ask for this money and, failing that, be a prick, to shove Jack's parenting failures in his face? Or was Jack to blame, expecting too much from Sebastian—reluctant to accept that his grown son was disillusioned and very different from the boy he had been? Clearly, he was less interested in the pursuits they used to share, and why not? Sebastian was now as riveted by surfing as Jack was to animation and video games. How to live was a matter constantly under construction by each wave of youth.

Late morning, two gringo surfers from California rolled up, wanting to be pulled out to one of the big breaks. Jack called his partner,

Rick, who drove the second jet-ski. They loaded up and headed for the beach, the surfers trailing behind in a rented Wrangler—both in their early thirties, if Jack had to guess. At that age, he'd hit his prime. Both had surfed big waves before, they said, strapping on their helmets: Fiji and Oahu, and Northern California. Far from shore, a gigantic swell arose at the break, higher and higher, until finally the wall came crashing down in a burst of white, the water exploding like snow tumbling in an avalanche.

The surfers moved with fluid ease as they stretched and warmed up in the sand. It took all of Jack's strength just to maneuver the jet skis off the ramp without clutching his shoulder in agony.

"You still get out there?" one of them asked.

"I wish," Jack said. "But I surfed my share of the big ones. Now I just hope I can keep up the jet-ski gig."

"Injury?" the other surfer asked.

"A few," Jack replied, and jabbed his thumb into his shoulder. "Could've moved down here earlier, maybe. But I had a wife, a kid. Mortgage, car payments." He paused. "You think you can do it all, or at least you try like hell."

The surfers nodded grimly.

They launched the jet-skis and towed the riders out. Each time the front of Jack's ski slammed down, water exploding, his joints howled. For the first few years living down here, he'd felt stronger and more elated than he'd felt since his twenties. This was how aging happened: in little blips of decline, like a motor sputtering out. The rushing swell arose, a wall of dark glass, the client's mop of hair and lean body an earlier version of himself. Had events taken a slightly different trajectory, he might have been pulling Sebastian out of the soup. Never had he fathomed that his son would ditch the sport completely, and Sebastian's doing so was, Jack hated to admit, a breathtaking disappointment. Jack circled away, engine vibrating, his chest growing warm beneath the snug life vest. The wave climbed to its peak and broke, the tiny figure flying down its slope. He sailed on and on, the surfer, until the wave finally collapsed on top of him, plunging him beneath for those long minutes below, the limbo underworld between this life and the next. Jack had once heard a quote by a famous poet, Basho—Japanese, if he recalled— who said the purpose of travel was not about seeing great sights, but in discovering the kindness of strangers in helping you out. At last the young man surfaced, gasping, and Jack whizzed by and tossed out the line. He cut the corner hard, spinning around, something he used to love to do for fun. Only today the impact was too hard, the pain instant and rocketing, and he gritted his teeth, squelched the cry in his throat.

*

A late afternoon storm drenched Jacó. Water gushed from the gutters, and the mechanics crossed themselves, praying for no mudslides in the hills where they lived. Gabi pedaled in from the Laundromat, and moments later, Sebastian padded downstairs, said the Internet was out. Gabi shut herself in the office and locked the door behind her. Jet-ski engine open, wrench in hand, Jack said, "Well, it ain't Tokyo. Let's go to dinner in town. We can try the WiFi there."

Sebastian ran his thin fingers over the ski's nose. Fresh coffee gurgled, the aroma cutting the shop dust; behind the office glass, Gabi bent over a ledger.

"How much you make hauling dudes out of the soup?" Sebastian asked.

"Five hundred a day. Why? You reconsidering vocations?"

"You just seem pretty happy here, that's all. You weren't the last time I saw you."

Jack turned the key in the ignition; the engine clicked rapidly but refused to start. The last visit with Sebastian had been in Florida, five years ago. Jack had been in crisis. Sebastian had helped him make the decision to retire early to Costa Rica and run a small, practical business for a steady income, so that he might surf before his knees and shoulders gave out as they were now. During that week in New Smyrna, he and Sebastian hit the beach at daybreak and again at sunset, packed up his house for the estate sale in between. Hell, Sebastian had been the one dragging *him* out of bed before dawn. How had he changed so much?

"This place has got to get boring, though," Sebastian said.

"Everywhere does, once you've been there long enough," Jack said. "But when the surf kicks up twenty feet, it ain't boring." Even as he said this, he tried to imagine life here without the waves, just puttering around above the shop and taking yoga class at one of the big hotels. He added, "It's you who's gotta keep the excitement going, discover new things. Be present. You never thought you'd see me as a mechanic, huh?" Sebastian laughed. The jet-ski fired up at last. He tossed his wrench on the table and grabbed a beer from the fridge. "Grab the laptop."

Even with ponchos and oversized umbrellas, all three got soaked on their way to the restaurant: Gabi's bangs plastered to her forehead, Jack's collar and sleeves stuck to his skin, and the bottom of Sebastian's jeans made soggy. He'd tried to roll them up but in vain; they were too tight. He had ditched the witchy boots for a pair of Jack's flip flops—tan Rainbows, decades old—from the pile without asking. The worn pair was Jack's most treasured, but he let this go. Gabi took the chair beside Jack, asked Sebastian something about the sushi in Japan. To Jack's relief, Sebastian launched into a fervent description of his neighborhood late-night sushi bar.

"But what you can't beat is their udon," he said. "Those noodles, I live for them."

Dinner arrived, tamales the size of Jack's hand, but Sebastian shook his head when Jack offered him some to try. Sebastian had ordered a Thai curry and talked on and on about Asia, how wonderful the high-speed trains were, how high-speed everything was everywhere, really. Gabi's eyes fluttered and her gaze drifted. Jack guessed Gabi knew where China and India were, and maybe Japan, but possibly not much more. She had never lived in a house with electricity until she'd moved in with him; Sebastian, of course, didn't know that. "Taking trips is fun but only if you have savings first," she'd said more than once.

"Funny, in all my corporate travels, I never made it to Japan," Jack said.

"So come." Sebastian nodded at Gabi, then added, "It's cold there, though. She wouldn't like it."

"How would you know what I would like?" she said, and sat up. "I'd like to see snow." She'd like to go to Argentina and film snowboarders, she said, if she could sell her surfing footage first. She elbowed Jack, grinning. "But maybe we could go to Japan instead."

Sebastian stared at the traffic creeping along in the pouring rain. "You know, you didn't have to wait for me to invite you to visit," he said. "I'm sure you still have plenty of frequent flyer miles in your account. It's not some big secret, me living in Tokyo."

"We'll see," Jack said. "I'd have to find someone to watch the shop." He excused himself for the restroom. He rounded the bar, and almost smacked into the grungy pack from the beach café. The blonde dreads, he noticed, somewhat hid the rough acne on the stocky surfer's cheekbone and forehead. A jutting canine broke his otherwise seamless grin.

He didn't want to admit to Sebastian, or to Gabi, let alone himself, but he didn't have any frequent flier miles left—those were long gone, spent in his other life, along with the rest of his past. The miscalculations and missteps he could do nothing to reclaim, and didn't know how to fix what remained—everywhere, everything he knew was unraveling toward decline. In the restroom mirror his face, sun-flecked and creased, reminded him of an old volleyball. Sebastian seemed to be coming around, at least. Maybe things weren't so bad.

When he returned, Gabi sat back, idly playing with her necklace; her nostrils flared. Sebastian was laughing at something across the street. "Check out those crackheads in the rain," Sebastian said, and pointed. There was still enough sunlight to see them through the sheets: a group of junkies who hung around near the casino, smoking crack all day long in the alleyway. The group was now attempting to climb the chain-link fence and reach the second-story of a closed nightclub, but every time one of them nearly reached the top, he lost his grip and fell back to the concrete.

"Out of their minds," Jack said, and sank into his seat with a huff. "Animals."

Sebastian whistled and the shrillness pierced through the muffle of the drumming rain. "HEY FELLAS!" he shouted. "NIGHTCLUB DOESN'T OPEN 'TIL MIDNIGHT!"

Drizzling raindrops beaded at the end of the table that fell outside the awning. Gabi squirmed and edged closer to Jack, who grimaced and opened his mouth to say something, then stopped. Had his son always had this obnoxious streak, and Jack hadn't been around enough to notice? Or had he just chosen not to? Or had some grudge triggered this behavior?

The waitress cleared their plates, brought the bill. Sebastian picked it up. "On me tonight," he said. He pulled out his wallet, thick with US twenties.

"But you don't have a job," Jack said. "What do you mean, it's 'on you'? Who's paying your way?"

Sebastian's face fell. "Does it matter? I'm paying for this."

"Yes, as a matter of fact, it matters greatly." Jack snatched the bill from Sebastian, lowered his voice. "When's the last time you had a job out there, if ever? I'm betting never, or you wouldn't be so goddam cavalier about everything. Let me guess: you're in Japan illegally. Didn't I raise you to be honest?"

"I don't know how you raised me," Sebastian said, his voice steely and even. "Mom did it."

"Oh, and your mother didn't raise you to lead an honest life, either? You're on a dangerous path, son, and living this way, having some sugar mamas pay for you, isn't going to get you anywhere."

"And what will? You're one to talk," Sebastian said. "Take a look around, where you've ended up. All those years you lived a life you pretended not to hate, with your big important 'real job,' and for what?"

Jack leaned in closer, the slip crumpling beneath his fingertips. "I made the most of what came my way, just like I'm making the most of living here. You could be making the most of this trip, but you haven't touched a board. And I don't understand it, because you loved being out there. Don't even try to pretend and say that was all fake. So why'd you give that up? I never even saw you doodle, and suddenly you're into animation?"

"You weren't there," Sebastian said abruptly, and louder. Gabi startled, grabbed Jack's leg under the table. "I drew all the time in high school, Mom took me to lessons, enrolled me in art camps."

Jack slumped back, drew his hands to his lap, the bill abandoned between them.

"I was in National Art Honor Society, did you know that? Probably not. When you came home, you didn't much ask what I was up to, just threw gifts at me and shoved photos of you playing Lawrence of Arabia or whatever in my face. You really didn't have a clue, did you?"

Jack opened his mouth, then closed it. "I'm sorry," he said. "No, I didn't." He tugged out his wallet, hands shaking, and counted out colones.

"Oh, right, my money's still not good enough," Sebastian said. "Nice. Hey, don't wait up for me." He arose, lifted the plastic bag with the laptop.

"Now hold on, we'll wait here and—"

"Fuck you, I do what I want." Sebastian charged out the back hallway of the restaurant. Moments later he darted across the street toward the Internet café, poncho misshapen and bright in the glare of headlights.

*

Neither of them said much on the way home. Jack popped in a surfing film but didn't even watch, Gabi beside him on the couch. Scissors pinched between her knees, she threaded glass beads onto elastic, making her bracelets. Jack tried to picture what their lives might have been like if he'd quit his career earlier and never moved to Costa Rica, but started a small business back in New Smyrna and spent more time with his young, impressionable son. If he hadn't been away so much, paid better attention when he was back home. Would that have mattered at all, or would Sebastian have turned out like this regardless—embittered, resentful? Was there a chance that his son might one day shake off his anger, forgive, and most importantly, take responsibility for his choices in life? See that losing oneself in casual arrangements and surface escapes wasn't an answer, but, in time, came with a steep, sometimes unforgiving, price? Jack hoped so, but there was no guarantee and little he could do. He guessed he would be there if Sebastian had a change of heart, and behavior. The young man might just have to hit rock bottom first.

Midnight, and still no sign or word from Sebastian. Jack slept fitfully. He dreamed first of the Pacific, a tsunami several stories high roaring toward Jacó. The dream happened at night but somehow he could see the wave clearly; it glowed with an eerie luminescence. In another, he paddled out to surf but when he tried to get back, he was stuck out there, drifting. Then another board floated past in the current—Sebastian rested on top, fully clothed but with his hands crossed on top of his chest, his paleness even more striking in death.

Jack jerked awake, sweating, his shoulder on fire. When the light hit his eyes Gabi was sitting up, shaking him awake. "He's not here," she said. "Sebastian."

"What?" Jack leaped up and hurried into the living area; the sheet lay scrunched at one end of the couch, untouched from the day before. "He never came home? Where the hell is he?"

"He's gone out the other nights," Gabi said, trailing him. "Maybe he didn't want to bother us, checked into a hotel." She said this weakly though, too far-fetched for belief.

"I don't think so." A moment passed, both of them just standing there. The coffee maker moaned; she shut it off. Jack rubbed his face. "Let's go look for him," he said.

They had begun to clumsily dress when Gabi clutched his arm. "Oh, no," she said. "The computer."

The Montero careened down the road to Jacó. When Jack reached the main street, he slowed and peered as far as the light shining from his headlights would allow. The tires crunched and sprayed rainwater. Mongrels meandered along the sidewalks, sniffing the litter here and there. He drove at a crawl all the way up to the Beatle Bar and the dive of a motel next door, where hookers brought their customers. A few prostitutes in tight clothing and heels staggered outside; embers glowed off cigarettes. One gringo, potbellied and sunburnt, lay passed out in the front seat of a rental car, door ajar and leg dangling to the pavement. A shrill voice shouted from a balcony, followed by raucous laughter. Jack slowed almost to a stop to get a better look. But no Sebastian.

"See anything?" he asked Gabi, his voice barely audible.

She shook her head, staring out the window, nails digging into her fists.

"You backed up your files, right? Like I showed you?"

"Some," she said. Her voice sounded thick.

Where the hell was the kid? The blood gushed in Jack's ears. Not far, probably passed out in some hotel room after-party or on the beach. So much for the laptop. He thought of all the dozens of hours of footage Gabi had taken over the past two years, standing and peering into the lens, and then the dozens of hours more that she'd spent learning the computer-editing program, all the instructions in English. Her family, the last time they had visited Nicaragua, had chided them for not bringing more goods that were difficult or costly to come by there: gauze and ointments for the medicine cabinet, name-brand lipstick, a DVD player and films, water filters. Her village with electricity that came on only for a few hours a day. How her mother had hugged Gabi and rocked her back and forth at the news of a big company showing interest in buying her daughter's surfing movies. Gabi's brothers were still selling cheap pottery to tourists down in Manuel Antonio, where Jack had met Gabi three years earlier.

This is unacceptable, Jack thought. If Sebastian had wanted to scream at him in that restaurant, Jack wouldn't have cared. But no, he ran out rather than tell Jack to his face everything that he'd been holding in all those years. *He was here, had plenty of chances to talk,* Jack reasoned. *When I catch him, I'm kicking him the hell out.*

The headlights lit up the shuttered cluster of storefronts by the casino, and a pair of skinny white legs—Sebastian, barefoot, as if waiting for them to pick him up. But as soon as Jack pulled up close enough to see his son's eyes and the twitching muscles of his face and elegant limbs, he knew what had happened, could picture the whole night from the Internet café to the Beatle Bar to the partying with the hookers at the no-tell motel. Behind Sebastian in the puddle-flooded alleyway, the crackheads crouched. They leaned back against the buildings, passed homemade pipes of aluminum foil back and forth.

Jack called out his name, but the shell that was his only son did not answer or even acknowledge the occupants of the truck. He called again, and this time Sebastian mumbled something in return. "The computer," Jack said. "Where is it?"

But Sebastian just stood there, arms akimbo and eyes roving back and forth. His flip flops, Jack's well-worn Rainbows, were nowhere to be seen. Jack idled there for another moment before pressing the gas and jerking back onto the road. They sped back to Autotica. Gabi wept silently. When they got home, dawn was just breaking behind the mountains, the skies clear.

Jack gathered all the flip flops and sandals that lay strewn on the mat outside the apartment and dropped them inside the door, except for Sebastian's boots, which were still damp and reeked faintly of mold. Then he collected Sebastian's belongings and his travel bag and left them in a heap outside the door, his flight itinerary tucked in the top of one of the boots. He locked the apartment, checked the door, and carried his surfboard down the stairs to where Gabi was waiting for him.

At Este Rios, the waves thundered and the deserted stretch of dunes gleamed like those of a distant moon. Gabi spread out a blanket, sank down and hugged her knees to her chest. The sand chilled Jack's feet even before he reached the water. Had he ever envisioned such a ruptured future? He wished he had made changes sooner, realized how emotionally neglected his wife and son must have been when Sebastian was in middle and high school. But he'd made the changes when he did, and even if he had screwed up as a husband and parent he had done some good elsewhere. Of all people, he had to believe in second chances. Gabi, he never would have met her if his marriage hadn't ended; she'd likely still be roaming the beaches selling her pottery and beaded bracelets—or worse. He'd claimed a different life, what his friends back home used to call "dropping out"; now they were fonder of the phrase "going off the grid," what his mechanics called "la pura vida." So many years he'd spent preoccupied with direct deposits, paying interest and premiums, and socking money into his IRA only to see so much melt away before his eyes as if all the money and hours worked and missed birthdays hadn't happened at all. But they had. To everything, there was a cost. Just hard to decipher what you were losing from inside the thick of it, much of the time.

He only caught a few waves before deciding to come in. He trudged up the dunes, squinting, the early light of dawn like twilight.

Where was the blanket? His pulse quickened, and for a moment he panicked—what if Gabi had gone? A shadow stirred, lumpen and animal-like; he hurried toward her. She used to sleep on the beach when she first arrived from Nicaragua, with only her backpack as a pillow. He cupped her head gently; she murmured. It didn't matter, he thought. He had chosen his life, and so had Sebastian. What could he do if his son, now grown, wanted to self-destruct? Stage an intervention, with no money for rehab?

The flock of scarlet macaws squawked above. Mornings, they feasted on nuts and fought in the treetops before moving on.

*

When they returned in the late morning, Sebastian's things were gone. Neither of them said anything. For a few days, they moved about the apartment gingerly, as if any moment, he might show up again, or they would stumble upon another valuable item missing: the iPod and docking station, Jack's old Tag watch, the weed or the cash they kept hidden in Gabi's sewing box. Jack locked the apartment even when he was down below, managing the mechanics and able to keep an eye on the stairs. He and Gabi grabbed lunch in Jacó, and Jack tried not to stare down the alleyways for too long, afraid the ghost of his son might still be lurking.

But a few more days passed, and then another week. Jack and Gabi picked out a new laptop at the RadioShack. At home, Jack booted up the machine and installed Skype. Sebastian's lime green icon glowed. He was alive—or at least online. But where?

Jack had dropped Gabi off at the laundromat to check the machines and she was not due back anytime soon. Thunder rumbled from the east, and the sunlight blotted to grey. Shoulder throbbing, he double-clicked on the green icon. One ring, then another. On the fourth, Sebastian answered.

"You're there," Jack said, and sat back. "What happened?"

Sebastian's video didn't come on, the camera icon remained with a red slash through it. Somewhere on the other end a young woman's voice whined in Japanese. Sheets rustled, and a toilet flushed in the background.

"Hey, are you there?" Jack paused. "Are you all right?"

"I'm fine."

"What happened to Gabi's computer?"

"I lost it, I guess," Sebastian said, voice flat. He sounded full of too much sleep or too little; Jack couldn't tell.

"This was our last time to surf together, you know that?" Jack said. His hand trembled as he tossed back three Ibuprofen. That morning he'd spent at the doctor's, scheduling his rotator cuff surgery the following month in San José. "I'm through."

"Is that right?" Sebastian replied. The Japanese woman said something, and Sebastian rattled off a few short lines in crisp Japanese before he said to Jack, "Sorry, I gotta go."

"You're not welcome in my house again," Jack said. Flecks of saliva beaded on the screen like raindrops. "In Costa Rica or anywhere else, not the way you're living. Do you get that?"

But the little green icon had bleeped away; he was speaking to no one now. His son's screen name stared back, a skeleton of characters in black and white.

CLÍNICA TIKAL

I had never heard of Clínica Tikal and probably never would have, if not for my trip to visit my grandmother and cousins in Guatemala. Although I always looked forward to returning to my parents' homeland, this trip felt different as soon as I stepped off the plane. For the first time, I arrived alone. Stinking traffic crawled from the airport to the outlying village; my eyes and throat burned from the diesel fumes and heat. The public buses stopped on the divided highway, and every hundred meters or so a parent with a small child in tow darted across the double lanes—common, I knew, for those living here, but I jumped every time and sucked in my breath. Just days ago, I was in New York City, hurrying down the subway escalators, late for class. "Turn left at the church with the baby Jesus in the box, and go three hundred meters," I instructed the cab driver— the address unchanged since I'd been born. Four years had passed since my last visit. The rustic houses of my abuela and relatives now struck me as grubby and poor, the loose dogs, many without tags, neglected. Chickens and goats darted before me as I strolled up the walk. For the first few days I forgot about the limited hot water, my showers running too long; embarrassed, I apologized, handed out the samples of shampoo and conditioner I'd brought as gifts. Still, my cousins called me "la Americana" so often that it played on me like a tired joke. I smiled weakly, all of us obviously trying to deflate the tension we felt—impossible to pretend that a life in the U.S. hadn't spoiled me.

Several days after my arrival, I paid a visit to Doña Emilia. For as long as I could remember, she had been close friends with my abuela—the visit all but required in coming back to the village, both a family obligation and a spiritual rite. Years later I would find out she was also a distant cousin. When I was little, I remember being afraid of the many chickens running around her yard. Some even wandered and clucked inside her house, scratching the dirt floor and pecking at fallen kernels of corn. Once, she handed me eggs, pale pastel and still warm. A special pair of hens lay the colored shells, she said; the eggs looked exactly like they had been dyed for Easter. I handed back the eggs and shrank away, transfixed not by the colors, but her magic—because how could she know? Her filmy, blind eyes each stared off in a different direction. Her clairvoyance had made her famous throughout the tiny country, and travelers journeyed from as far away as Mexico and Costa Rica to seek her predictions. She had warned a former president who sought her guidance not to ride in a certain black car because she saw his death, but he ignored her warning. Two weeks later they pried his body out of the front seat, the assassin's bullet through his brain and his blood on the road.

I knew all the stories from my family members about the accuracy of her predictions, in one way or another. She had foretold my mother having twins and my parents' divorce before they had married. When I was a little girl, she had seen me as a young woman in a city with snow on the sidewalks and tall silver buildings reaching to a grey sky. And so I didn't argue when my grandmother told me Doña Emilia was expecting me, maybe because I was a little curious about what the seer might say about my next steps in New York. Besides, she never charged—she claimed that clairvoyants who did had impure intentions—so at least I didn't have any money to lose by visiting with her.

On that afternoon I sat on Doña Emilia's porch in a homemade rocking chair made of old wire hangers and plastic twine. The inside of her house—concrete block walls, dirt floor, and tin roof—stunk of burnt coffee, chicken droppings, and the tamales that she baked over an open fire and peddled on the street. A few years ago I would have thought nothing of the way she lived, and perhaps laughed at her as she chanted under her breath, shuffling down the street with her hamper of tamales. Now I teetered on the rocker's edge, shoulders squared, as her rough hands traced my face, and a swath of grey hair mingled with mine as she leaned close. I caught the scent of her body odor—earthy, acrid—and held my breath. She pressed her thumb just above the bridge of my nose, on my forehead. Then her hand drifted down to my right side, grazed my abdomen. For a long moment afterward, we sat in silence. She had never taken so long to read me before; from the time I was thirteen, she had always rattled off the boys I should avoid by the time her hands left my skin. "Never ride on the back of a motorcycle," she had warned before my senior year of high school, "and keep away from the boys who do." My homecoming date was killed shortly after graduation, after exiting a highway ramp too fast. Coincidence, perhaps, but too sobering to be ignored.

"What's wrong?" I finally blurted out. "I'm not pregnant."

She cracked a wide grin of grey teeth. "No, you're not," she said. "But you have a cyst on your ovary."

"Is it dangerous?"

"If you don't remove this, it will keep growing," she said. "And you won't be able to have children."

My gaze fell to my lap, and I bit my thumbnail. I had always seen myself having several children.

She sat back. "There is a clinic far from here, but very good. You will have to take a bus."

"Shouldn't I change my ticket and fly back?" Even as I said this, my thoughts raced ahead to New York. I would be back in less than two weeks and could see a doctor there. But a procedure like this would be expensive. I could not afford insurance and so did not have any. As a rule, medical care was much cheaper in Latin America; the doctors often trained in the U.S. or Europe, and the hospitals were just as good, if not better.

"I have very little money," I said. "Why can't I go to a doctor nearby, or in Guatemala City?"

She pressed a spot on my lower abdomen where I guessed my ovary, and the cyst, must be. "You must remove it now, before you go back. No waiting—it's growing fast. If it bursts, you'll be in a lot of pain." She reached up and touched my forehead once again, between the brows. "You go to the ordinary doctors, you spend the rest of your trip in Guatemala City. Where I am sending you, they give excellent care, I promise. Truly, they are the best."

I had experienced no pain, no blood, no sign of anything wrong. What if she was wrong, and there was no cyst? I had nothing to lose, I supposed. Yet how could a clinic which Doña Emilia called the best afford to give free medical care? This was a question I did dare to ask.

"Your care will cost nothing, no need to worry. But you must tell no one where you are going—they insist on keeping very discreet," she said. "Bring nothing but your pajamas, a small bag. You will stay there for several days."

How could she see inside me, read my body and my thoughts? I didn't like this at all. "Nadie? Am I supposed to lie?" I asked. "Not even tell my grandmother?"

"Tell them you are going to Tikal, that you want to see the ruins there. Then no one will bother you with questions. All you have to pay is the bus fare."

The screen door creaked. I said nothing. Even if I flew back to New York, I would have to wait weeks to get the procedure, and how would I pay for it? While here was this clinic probably run by the Red Cross or one of the many Christian charities throughout Latin America. I could get this tumor removed now, free and clear—I wanted it out of my body. "Gracias, Doña," I said. I leaned over and kissed her on both cheeks. She gave me a card with the name of the facility: *Clínica Tikal*—no phone number listed, just the physical directions. I bristled, not about to ride a stinky bus across the countryside for six hours, risk losing my purse to bandidos at the likelihood of a roadside robbery, just to find the clinic wasn't up to standard after all, have to turn around and go back. I held out the card and said, "Where's the phone number? Don't I need to make an appointment?"

Doña Emilia climbed to her feet, shooed a hand over the card. "Do you think the poor Indians who need treatment pick up a phone? You just show up, híja." Then she disappeared into her hut. I stood still for a moment, realizing I had all but insulted her by doubting her advice. When I peered through the doorway Doña Emilia was crouched over a bucket, drawing out the water inside with a teacup and splashing it over her arms. She chanted something under her breath as she did this, her cleansing ritual which she performed after every reading before she moved on to another task. She wouldn't even come to the door to sell a single tamale until she had finished.

At my grandmother's house, I packed a light bag with my overnight items and a change of clothes. When I approached my abuela and asked where I could buy a ticket for the bus to Tikal and El Remate, the name of the village nearest the clinic, she took the card and turned it over, even though she couldn't read. "I'm going to see the famous ruins," I said, hoping she didn't pick up the waver in my voice. I was prepared for her to ask questions, but she did not. I had just returned from Doña Emilia's, after all, and who knew what the clairvoyant had said? A meeting with such a powerful seer remained a secret unless the visitor wanted to divulge Doña's findings. And many didn't.

I purchased the ticket at the corner store and boarded the bus the next morning, the aisle and seats crowded with gringo backpackers and the rest who looked like me: the high cheekbones, slanted eyes, wide foreheads. Only my skin was the color of pale corn, thanks to the dark Manhattan winters. As the bus bumped up and down the roads and swerved to avoid the peasants and their cattle, I probed my lower abdomen in the spot where Doña Emilia had touched me. But even when I pressed hard, I felt no pain. Had I had acted too quickly, hopping on this bus for a surgery, with no phone service? Perhaps I should have made an appointment with a doctor in Guatemala City first, to make sure that Doña Emilia had been right. The bus lurched to a stop, and a woman sat down beside me. Her hair was twisted into a long rope that swayed below her waist, her scalp thin from years of pulling the sections tight. Had I not been back for so long that my happy memories created a romanticized version of Guatemala, of getting a reading on the psychic's porch? Had my longing to fit in here so badly with my extended family prompted me to momentarily lose the savvy reasoning and worldliness I'd gained in New York? I could hear my city friends laughing, even now. But too late. I edged over, gulped what fresh air I could at the open window. The mountains lay ahead, the terrain now completely unfamiliar to me. I had never traveled to this part of Guatemala—Petén, the province which borders Mexico.

El Remate, I discovered, was as far north as I could travel by bus. The limestone ruins of Tikal, one of the largest cities of the ancient Mayan civilization, lay within the rainforest, forty miles from where the bus dropped me off. To get closer to the ruins themselves, I would need to take one of the smaller tourist vans. I wondered if, depending on my condition, the clinic would permit me to explore the World Heritage site—at least that would make the long trip more worthwhile. In El Remate, I showed the card and the locals shook their heads at me. Then I remembered how few of them could read. I asked a shop owner. Clínica Tikal, he said, was not as far away as the ruins but on the edge of the national park, several kilometers outside of town. He instructed me to look for the sign on the side of the road and follow the dirt lane back into the jungle.

By the time I hiked to the hand-painted wooden sign with an arrow pointing the way to a driveway lined with dried cattle dung, I wanted to give up. My throat ached for water, and my temples throbbed with a headache from the bus's diesel fumes. Why wasn't this clinic centrally located in El Remate, where locals and travelers both could have easy access to medical care? Unless this was one of those new holistic health centers—but no, only gringos with dollars had access to such places. I slowed my pace. What if this clinic had been established in such a remote place to care for indigenous villagers with serious diseases, such as tuberculosis and cholera?

At last I rounded the bend and Clínica Tikal came into view: half a dozen concrete block buildings like any other common structure in Latin America. Children laughed and kicked a soccer ball to one another. I climbed the concrete steps of the building marked OFICINA, counting how many indigenous patients rested in rockers underneath the porches of the outbuildings. Twenty, maybe more.

Inside the office a young woman around my age sat behind a desk. A small fan blew the loose hair away from her face as she sewed a rosette onto a baby's christening dress. I told her that Doña Emilia had sent me, and I needed a surgery to remove a cyst from my ovary. After I completed a few simple forms, she said that I must be tired and hungry if I had come from so far away. She motioned for me to follow her.

On the footpath we passed a few nurses—if that's who they were; I saw no one in uniform—entering and exiting rooms, pulling curtains shut behind them. Inside, patients reclined on their beds or in chairs, slept or stared. No TVs to watch, or books to read. No mosquito netting, either—were they not afraid of malaria, zika, dengue fever? She led me to a plain, private room with a cot and two windows facing a stand of banana trees outside. Minutes later, I was sipping from a cracked coconut and nibbling slices of fresh mango, alongside a small portion of white fish and rice. I felt much better. I asked about seeing the doctor, and she urged me to rest from my journey, that I would meet the doctor tomorrow. She left, and immediately after came the rains in great heavy sheets, the footpaths swiftly turning into shallow pools.

The rains stopped but the sun had still not set when I changed into my pajamas and crawled into bed. The lights flickered off, and back on—rolling brown-outs, possibly to conserve electricity. Had there been solar panels on the roof? As evening descended, the silence grew palpable. I heard none of the noises which usually filled doctors' offices and hospitals: no quick footsteps, no crying outbursts, no humming generators or beeping equipment. I detected no sharp odor of disinfectant or sickness, only the dank undergrowth of the jungle and afternoon rain. Fresh air—maybe that was the point. Nothing else struck me as remarkable. Why had Doña Emilia insisted that this clinic was the best? Because they did not charge? The young woman had brought me to this room, but no one had stopped by to check my vital signs—who were the plain-dressed staff going in and out of rooms, if not nurses? Surely they didn't only have medical personnel here during the day? I made a mental note to ask the doctor just which aide organization funded Clínica Tikal.

*

I fell asleep, exhausted from the bus and the heat, my dreams sweeping and vivid. I was climbing ruins that I guessed to be Tikal. The doctor wanted to perform the operation at night, atop a temple. The heavens gleamed more than the Manhattan skyline, more spectacular than anything I'd ever seen before. I felt consoled by the stars, knowing that's where I had come from and where I would one day return; I was made from their dust, and everything else I knew; I didn't want to come down, but I must.

"You will have three children," the doctor told me, but he wasn't the doctor anymore. He was Doña Emilia, the moon reflecting in the clouds of her eyes. Then she reached out and clasped my face.

In the morning a breakfast tray of arepas and fruit greeted me. On the edge of my bed sat the man I supposed must be my doctor, peeling and eating a banana. He wore no scrubs and seemed like an ordinary middle-aged Latino man, slight of build, his small ears half-hidden by dark hair in need of a trim. Dressed in jeans and a collared shirt, he didn't appear like a doctor; then again I wasn't quite sure how a doctor in a clínica rustica was supposed to look. But I liked the way he sat there, one knee crossed over the other, eating the wild banana which he'd probably picked from the tree outside, without a care in the world. When he finished, he tossed the peel out the open window. "So Doña Emilia sent you?" he asked, more of a statement than a question. "What did she tell you about us?"

"Not much," I said. "Just that you are the best place for surgery in Guatemala. I hope she's right." I rearranged the pillows and propped up higher in the bed, adding, "My backside is killing me from that bus trip. The roads could use some work around here."

He smiled. "I like your sense of humor," he said.

"I just want this cyst out, okay? If she's right about it existing at all."

He instructed me to lie flat on my back while he felt around my lower abdomen. Doña Emilia had been correct to send me here, and not a moment too soon, he said. If I hadn't felt pain yet I would likely be doubled-over in a few days, unless he removed the cyst. Then he proceeded to instruct me about the procedure.

"We do things differently here than anywhere else, certainly any place you'd go in the States," he said. "For instance, nearly all the medicines and remedies we give to our patients are from the surrounding forests, everything natural, to purge toxins and restore health—as the rest of the so-called medical establishment has yet to accept. And we don't use anesthesia."

I sat forward, clutching the top of the light blanket which covered me up to my waist. "But I don't want to be awake while you cut me open," I said. I thought of Tikal, of the Mayans who once cut out the beating hearts of those they sacrificed.

"Please don't worry," he said. "You'll be awake, but you'll feel no pain. That I promise you. We have other methods." Finished and apparently satisfied with his probing, he resumed his seat at the foot of my bed. Then he cautioned me about the recovery period. While this surgery produced minimal scarring and posed the least risk for damaging the ovary, the procedure required that I take extreme caution with myself for six to eight months afterward. When I asked why, the doctor's expression and tone changed from lighthearted to serious. He explained that with a standard operation to remove an ovarian cyst, I would be almost fully recovered after ten days. But this surgery was a different type. I would need to behave as if I had just been operated on for at least six months, even after I felt like myself again—no heavy lifting or working out of any kind. "Think of it as restoring balance to a system," he said. "You want to treat yourself delicately, not only because the cyst will be removed, but so that you may heal and not have it grow back."

I nodded. The whole thing seemed to make perfect sense and, at the same time, struck me as odd. What kind of surgical method could be so delicate? *Lasers*, I thought. That must be what he was going to use. No anesthesia, a fine procedure, minimal scarring. And of course, the surgery would be happening in another part of the facility, where they had equipment, and not this barren room. My face flushed, and I felt almost silly for not realizing this sooner.

"So I will need your consent to operate tomorrow," he said. "Any more questions?"

"I guess not," I said. A woman on staff came by with coconut water, said to drink. The doctor waved goodbye and disappeared out the door. Not until I had finished most of the drink did I realize that I had forgotten to ask the name of the aide organization in charge of the clinic, nor had I signed a consent form. The doctor, he hadn't introduced himself—possibly we both had forgotten. And yet I had felt in his presence a complete sense of trust.

*

I dozed off again, and when I woke, wished I had brought a book, and there was nothing to read in my room. So I decided to go in search of a magazine, and to further explore the property. Once again, the children kicked their soccer ball through the mud, the older patients who rested on chairs outside looking on, apparently unperturbed. None of them were hooked up to IVs or monitors as you would see at a modern medical facility. But once in a while, staff members brought around trays with boiling water, mugs and loose tea in jars, tall glasses of dark juice, thick with pulp, or coconut water—were these natural replacements for IV fluid? The patients said a few words to one another, now and then, but seemed to rest more than anything. I heard no cries of pain or bedside grief coming from any of the rooms or buildings. Nor did I see any large crosses or portraits of the Virgin Mary hung on walls. If the clinic had no connection to the Church or any Christian organization, who funded this place, and why?

Then I wondered if the man I'd spoken with earlier was one of those fake doctors I'd seen exposed on cable TV shows, the kind of snake oil salesmen who scammed their living from sick people in the Third World—so-called doctors who hid a chicken liver in the palm of one hand and kneaded a patient's abdomen with the other, then pretended to pull out a diseased organ from the flesh. But then, why wouldn't the clinic charge? And the doctor, whoever he was, had struck me as warm, congenial; he had steady eye contact, a practiced and professional manner. A hoax—no. Nor had I gotten the impression that this doctor had been preoccupied with making his new BMW payment while he'd spoken with me, one eye tracking the time, unlike doctors I had gone to in New York, who saw patients every fifteen minutes.

When the children sailed the soccer ball in my direction, I jumped up and joined them. They squealed and played a game of keep-away with the ball, me stuck in the middle, their little chests heaving and brows glistening with sweat. "You don't seem very sick," I asked one little boy during a lull. "What's the name of your doctor?" But the boy just stared up at me blankly before running away. A gigantic kapok tree extended over the middle of the yard, and howler monkeys lumbered overhead. I approached one child after another, but each refused to speak. Instead, the mood of the game turned. As I headed for the ball, a little girl stuck out her foot to trip me and I stumbled to regain my balance. Only after I sank into the rocker underneath the porch that I considered how I must appear to these children. Despite my Guatemalan features, nothing else about me belonged here. The way I walked, my salon-treated hair and nails, my Ralph Lauren jeans—all told this world I was an outsider.

The burst of activity reminded me of the doctor's warning the day before. No heavy lifting or physical activity for six months. Did this mean I would not even be able to lift my suitcase from the curb to my apartment? What about the big shoulder bag I carried in the city? Most days I stood for hours, walked countless blocks. Would I need to rely on others for help—with groceries, and to go up steps? Move back in with my parents? I scolded myself for not asking the doctor more questions when given the opportunity. Now I wasn't sure what I might be giving up by having the surgery here. For how many days would I remain at this clinic, exactly? I probably wouldn't get to see the ruins at Tikal after all, unless I went that afternoon.

To my right a wrinkled woman sat in a rocker, weaving a brightly colored bag. "How far to the ruins of Tikal?" I asked her.

"It is too far," she said, without looking up.

"If I walk to the road, could I find a van to take me there today?"

She shifted in her rocker, but her hands didn't stop moving. "So many people like you come here just to visit Tikal," she said. "Tell me, what is so compelling about an old city, except to show yourself that even the biggest cities will one day die out? No one will ever live there again, but here—we are living." She smoothed the pattern and slowly nodded to herself, smiling.

I headed back to my room, uneasy. Across the yard, two older men, maintenance workers, tended a garden. Sunlight broke through the trees, but the complex remained sleepy, quiet. Room after room I passed, and yet still saw no modern medical equipment. I passed a kitchen where a half-dozen women chopped greens and ground substances I couldn't see with mortars and pestles. Kettles boiled atop a stove. The women, some of whom I recognized from their rounds— carrying trays on the walkways, ducking in and out of rooms—spoke softly to one another. They fell abruptly silent when I paused before the doorway. I hurried on and, having found nothing to read, climbed back into bed. Soon the rains poured again, and nightfall brought a damp chill. Underneath the blankets, I shuddered.

*

The next morning, soon after daybreak, the doctor entered my room. Three women and two men accompanied him; I guessed they must be his assistants, although I wondered why he needed so many of them for a relatively simple operation. One of them carried a silver tray, simple and stainless-steel; it may have belonged to a dentist office, though I didn't think anything of the tray at the time. None of them wore a surgical mask, gloves, or smock, although by now I had stopped questioning the everyday clothes worn by the clinic workers; in three days, I hadn't spotted a single smock. Maybe they were going to escort me elsewhere. But as soon as the group entered my room, something shifted both around and within me, and I sensed that here we would remain. The atmosphere felt somewhat like after an auditorium has emptied out after a great performance. This energy enveloped me like the sun's light, danced over my insides. This warmth swept to the center of my chest and gently rested there.

The doctor stood over me, on the side of my body where he was to remove the cyst. He greeted me and introduced the others as his assistants. The woman who carried the tray now fetched a stand from the corner, arranged the stand beside my bed and placed the tray on top of it.

"In a few moments you won't be able to move, but this paralysis will only be temporary," he said. "You will remain awake but relaxed. Do you understand?"

I nodded. I had never felt more awake in my life. The assistants positioned themselves around the sides of my bed. Once in a circle, they bowed their heads and clasped hands. A sound filled the room like nothing I had ever heard before. High-pitched, yes, but not a sound which came from a mouth or throat, but from within themselves, like the communication of bats. And I could no longer move except for a slight tilt of the head, just enough to look down and watch the doctor part the bed sheet. He folded my loose nightshirt and pants down and back. One of the assistants raised the silver tray and held it up for the doctor, its empty surface catching the light from the bulb above and the glare momentarily blinding me. Was that where they were going to deposit the removed cyst?

My body felt heavier and heavier, almost as if I was hovering above everything, and my heart beat as if I were watching the events about to happen to someone else. But then the doctor appeared to pick up an invisible instrument from the silver tray. He hesitated for a moment over the skin of my lower abdomen, his fingers pinched together as if he held a pencil or a razor blade. Then in one swift motion, he flicked his wrist and I felt something cut through my skin. I felt the instrument slide into my body even though I could see nothing in his grasp. I felt no pain, only the instrument prodding around. All this time, the otherworldly sound filled the room and must have echoed throughout the whole complex of buildings, through the jungle, into space—almost insect-like, perhaps how a plague of descending locusts must sound.

The procedure only lasted a few minutes, during which I never spotted a drop of blood nor an open cut. The doctor did not hold up a chicken liver like a prize trophy or say anything to me until it was over, when he placed the invisible instrument once again back on the silver tray and asked me how I felt; the main assistant set down the tray on the stand. She and the tray were partially blocked by the doctor, and I strained for a better view. I thought I spotted something tiny and flesh-toned on the gleaming surface. "I feel fine," I told him, then looked again and saw nothing, just the empty tray. The trilling noise stopped; the assistants stepped back, lifted their heads and filed out the door as silently as they had entered. The woman who had brought the tray swiftly replaced the stand in the corner as she exited, carrying the tray before her. This left the doctor and me alone.

As soon as they had departed, the full feeling and mobility of my body returned along with an extreme exhaustion. When I reported this to the doctor, he said my body was repairing itself.

"Remember what I told you. Nothing strenuous for at least six months."

I asked if the cyst had been removed completely, and he said yes. Then I asked about what I'd just heard and seen, and if he and the others were not from this world.

The doctor's face softened, and from the crinkles at his eyes and mouth I realized he must have been older than I had first thought. He shook his head. "Every one of us is from Flores or El Remate, or another village nearby," he said. "But many years ago, our people were visited by advanced beings—wonderful beings." He went on to explain that the beings had passed along techniques of higher consciousness and healing, knowledge about energy and natural remedies, as well as warnings about the toxic practices of the out-side world, including Western medicine.

Of course, I asked why these beings hadn't shared this knowledge with more of the world—why many more such places didn't exist, if this were true.

"They do exist," he said, "in remote places, areas with the worst poverty and disease. Why would these beings not come to these places first, to those the rest of the world has abandoned so completely? They came to this place because they knew the people would receive them with gratitude and love." He glanced out the window. Raindrops splashed off the banana leaves, and somewhere nearby a rooster crowed.

He left. A few minutes later a nurse entered with some herbal tea, and as I sipped the hot, tart water, I wondered about what I had just seen and heard and felt, how after such a routine surgery I had not expected to feel both stunned with an immeasurable stillness and transformed throughout my whole being. I thought of New York City, and how the place now seemed like a nonsensical steel-and-concrete maze that I wasn't sure I wanted to make my home but would return to in just a few days. The kids ran, shouting, and now and then the soccer ball thudded against a concrete wall. I laid back, closed my eyes. As the rain pattered within the trees, I drifted to sleep.

*

I remained at Clínica Tikal just one more day. On the long, crowded, nauseating bus ride back I examined the faces of the passengers. How many of them knew about the wonders of Clínica Tikal? Perhaps the clinic had been around for so long, and buried so deeply in this remote province, that the locals didn't consider such medical practices to be wonders at all?

The bus clattered into the village at dusk. I intended to see Doña Emilia once more before my flight back to New York—why not now? This time I climbed her porch steps unannounced. Inside, stone scraped against stone; before an open window Doña Emilia stood, grinding her cornmeal by hand with a roller against a slab. Slowly she turned over her shoulder, asked, "Who's there?" I told her it was me, and that I had returned from the clinic. "Has the cyst been removed?" I asked, stepping forward. "The procedure—it was unusual. I need to know."

She wiped her hands on her skirt, shuffled toward me. "Why do you doubt?" she asked.

"Please, I need to know—if everything is okay. If I'll be able to have children." I took her hand and placed it on my abdomen, in the same spot she'd prodded before.

Her fingers rested there a few moments, then fluttered back to her side. "Sí," she said. "You are healed completely."

"I am? But nothing's—damaged? My children will be normal?"

"They instructed you on how to take care of yourself?"

I sank onto the stool nearby, and nodded.

"Then why would you have anything to worry about? Unless you don't listen." She clasped my cheeks in her hands and pressed her crinkled forehead against mine. "But you will."

She stepped away and I could still feel her papery skin against mine. The heat from her cooking fire warmed my arms and neck as she bent over and dropped two logs onto the flames. "But why?" I asked. "Why did this happen to me—to be cured this way?"

"Did you not want to be cured?"

"Of course. Just—I don't understand how they healed me. I always thought I wanted to believe in magic, that to see a miracle— to have one happen to me—would be amazing. I didn't expect to feel this scared."

"Ah!" she exclaimed, with a little laugh. "It is completely normal to feel as you do. You can never go back to not knowing what greater powers are at work, here and in other realms." Smoke curled from the fire. She felt for the roller and the slab, spread corn from a bucket, resumed her work. "But, even if you are so bothered, there is no need to think of this again. Just know that you are well, and be grateful."

"I wish that were enough."

She spoke to me then, said that when her third eye had pressed against mine, that she had seen I would have a good life. That I would soon meet a light-spirited and adventurous man, and fall in love. When I arose, the scent of roasting corn overwhelmed me.

"Gracias," I told her, as we hugged goodbye upon her porch. "I'll try not to think any more about it. Except—have you been there?"

She spat on the uneven boards, hiked her dress above her knees, and sank back into her rocking chair. "Nunca," she said. "I have no need. My work is here."

*

In my grandmother's pueblo, the bustle of daily life startled me back into the world. My bus had returned at nightfall; the next morning my abuela arose at dawn and stood for hours, grinding her cornmeal by hand just like Doña Emilia had. The next-door neighbor, an elderly man, hacked the encroaching jungle by himself all day, sunlight glinting upon the machete as he wielded it overhead. "He's ninety-three," my grandmother told me. In the United States I would never believe a person of such an advanced age capable of clearing an acre with a machete. Yet here this man was. Although some of the elderly inhabitants of New York stood out for other reasons: their bright, flashy outfits, their sturdy strides that kept pace with the flood of pedestrians on the sidewalks, a chatty zest for life. I was about to tell my grandmother this, but then stopped. How to explain a whole world, and one so alien?

Before I had a chance, my grandmother asked me to describe the ruins of Tikal. She had never traveled beyond Guatemala City. Those she knew who had gone to Tikal had told her that the pyramids must have been made by God, or angels; they did not believe humans, centuries ago, could have built such structures from stone. What did I think?

"It's true: what I saw there was difficult to believe" I said, and paused. "But going there did change my perception, gave me a greater faith in what is possible. Angels—is that what people think?"

"Where are your pictures?" she asked.

Under the banana tree, my younger cousins darted and collected eggs; my aunt chatted away on her cell phone. I said that, in my hurry, I had forgotten my camera. To myself I thought, *Someday I'll return to Tikal, maybe with my husband and children, and climb the ancient steps.* From dust to dust, the priests say, but they never admit what the poet meant: dust, not merely of earth, but stardust. And I won't be afraid to tell my children this, when I show them the heavens at night: where we came from, where we'll one day go back. You, me, the stone slabs—we all reach our glory, then crumble back to cosmic ash.

*

Not long after, I met my husband, as predicted, and moved to south Florida. He was an American entrepreneur who owned a string of small factories throughout Central and South America, a sandal-making company. I had never told anyone about my experience at the jungle clinic, not even my husband, and the memory took its place with the other strange tales of my family's village, until one day when I went to my doctor's office for a routine exam. I had been married for less than a year and was pregnant with my first child. During the ultrasound, I asked the technician, "Can you check my ovaries?" I shifted my weight and craned my neck forward to glimpse the screen. I could make out nothing.

But a moment later the technician exclaimed, "When did you have surgery on your ovary? You must have had a cyst."

"A long time ago," I said. "I was in college." I rested my head against the cool paper sheet. I had thought seldom of Clínica Tikal, though the invisible scalpel and that piercing, unmistakable sound had been branded forever into my memory—the experience so bizarre, I preferred to forget it. "How could you tell?" I asked. "Is something wrong?"

"Just that whoever performed the surgery did an excellent job," she answered. "I can barely detect any scarring, it's so minimal. See?" She pointed out my ovary on screen, and I peered forward once again. "Where did you get this done?" she asked.

"Guatemala," I said, and lay back.

"Really?" she said, and her eyebrows shot up. Then she proceeded to tell me details of the fetus, and the past fell away.

On the drive home I contemplated the news of the baby—a girl. Alone, part of me was pulled elsewhere: to that jungle compound, the card void of a telephone number, the doctor whose name I didn't know. I had imagined none of it. Did such a place still exist? Did I want to find out? How could I feel gratitude and relief for what those who ran the clinic did for me, and at the same time, even years later, a gripping fear? Maybe the mysterious, even if beautiful and natural, must also terrify. Maybe such terror—the same terror that accompanies childbirth and death—is a kind of humility, an awe. Would life feel so precious without it?

Years later, we live part-time in Escazú, Costa Rica, my husband, three children and me. Our house is one of dozens in a compound, guarded by dim-witted men in blue uniforms who operate the gate, patrol the grounds, and do little else; I suppose they keep us safe. I enjoy cheering my children in their soccer matches and wrapping tamales in banana leaves with them on weekends. My abuela died three months ago, on the heels of Doña Emilia's passing. I have still not gone back to Tikal, and could almost believe the experience did not happen at all.

Only the other night I was washing dishes long after the maids had left. My husband was upstairs, putting the children to bed. Through the open windows and over the dim chorus of insects, a sound arose—a high-pitched, collective trill. I stepped outside. The breeze rustled the trees; the clouds drifted and parted over the moon. I crept upstairs, short of breath, and slipped in my daughter's room. She lay still, already asleep, her chest rising and falling in measured rhythm, her small body firm beneath the quilt.

SPLITTING THE PEAK

Russell Scott wakes before six. Dawn casts the bungalow's interior in a golden haze, illuminating the dust which hovers mid-air like bursts of sea spray. He pads into the living room. The half dozen surfboards resting on the rack catch shafts of morning light, plastered with worn and bumpy wax. The computer screen *ohms* to sea-blue life. He checks the surf report. Overnight, the ocean has kicked up a notch, and the breeze slaps the palm branches against the windows. It's August, and a tropical storm is gathering in the Atlantic, making tracks from the Caribbean for Florida's eastern beaches. If it turns into a hurricane, he and Audrey will have to evacuate again to her folks' in Orlando. But it's still early in the season, and he hopes that the storm will remain far out and just sizable enough to kick up some overhead swells for the next week. The prospect of retreating inland with Audrey doesn't really faze him, though, because he knows Heidi Sierra is back in Florida until the end of the month.

The flood of sunlight heckles him out for his early morning session. But he clicks off the surf report and pulls up the website he's memorized over the last several days: *Sierra's Surfer Chicas— Come Catch a Wave with Us in San Juan del Sur, Nicaragua.* On the next page, Heidi Sierra's face beams back, her grin the same as he remembers, only decorated with tiny crinkles at the corner of her mouth and eyes like starbursts. He navigates his email, reopens the message from the social networking site he rarely uses but where, somehow, Heidi Sierra has found him. He scans the brief message again: "Russell, are you still in Florida? I'm up until the 31st from Nica. Would love to get together." He tries to escape the screen, glances at the shortboards awash in white light, asks himself which one he'll ride for today's sunrise session, but Heidi's presence on the screen yanks him back. The cursor blinks in the blank Reply box, and her days-old message remains unanswered.

The sunlight strikes the screen with a temporary blinding glare, blotting out Heidi's grin, her question, and the day's report like an eclipse.

*

Before his first year as a pro surfer had kicked off, he would often wake up startled to find Audrey sleeping next to him, the phenomenon of teenage years spent waking up on a strange couch in some industry rep's living room or in a foreign hotel, needing a few moments to figure out his whereabouts—why they called the Junior Pro circuit "the Grind." But he liked the easiness of these hours with no catalogue shoots or heats to harass him out of bed, nothing but Audrey's tousled brown hair and warm, slender arms and the surf a few blocks away. And the sex, until Audrey scrambled out from the covers and shoved him aside, giggling as she hurriedly dressed. She was studying at Florida Atlantic University, so she could be near him on his visits home from the tour. One of her classes was creative writing, and after the first week she carried a Mead notebook with her everywhere, the cover splitting away from the spirals, the exercises given by the instructor her new preoccupation. Sometimes Russell came back from the beach to find her staring off and scrawling away—not terribly surprising, considering her love of books. He was more curious about the close readings the professor assigned, and while Audrey sprawled beside him on the beach, writing, he would tug out the latest photocopied story.

"Katherine Mansfield," he said one morning. "Who's that?"

"Oh! She's great," Audrey said, barely looking up. "I think you'd like her stories, seeing as how you've spent so much time in that part of the world." When he responded with a puzzled stare, Audrey added, "She was from New Zealand. Died at twenty-four."

"You're kidding," he muttered, and began reading. The white noise of the surf filled his ears, the sun suspended high overhead. After a life in motion—tromping on and off planes, modeling beachwear, paddling out just so the ocean could propel him back towards shore—he relished stillness. Nothing was expected of him; the hours melted and ran together like wax. Lying there, traveling wherever you wanted to go in your own mind, no wordy explanations required—it was perfection. A longing stirred inside him for the parallel life that eluded him: studying together with Audrey at the university library, listening to renowned speakers, having impassioned discussions, not only with her but with classmates and professors.

He would not see Audrey for four months, until after the Billabong Pro in Tahiti.

*

R. Scott and H. Sierra. They were booked side-by-side in business class, Honolulu to Sydney. The year-long WSL Championship Tour awaited them at Snapper Rocks, Bells Beach, the Banzai Pipeline, Honolua Bay. Barely twenty, all he knew of Heidi was that she had already claimed two titles in her debut as a pro. They exchanged introductions and settled into their headphones and magazines until, three hours in and restless, dinner trays piled with crumbled foil and napkins, they struck up conversation. Heidi Sierra leaned forward, one wispy tail of her blonde Swiss Miss braids grazing his biceps. She jutted her paperback in front of him, *Tapping the Source*— a surf classic he recalled reading back in eighth grade—and asked about the novel he was reading, *The Heart of the Matter*—he was in a Graham Greene phase.

"It's about expats in Africa, but it's a love story, too. I guess." Russell offered it to her.

"Let me guess. About two people who can't be together the way they want to." Heidi glanced over the cover, eyebrows arched. "The depressing ones are the only kind of love story ever worth telling. Romeo and Juliet, no one wants to hear about them finding each other as best friends with a bunch of passions in common. Can you tell I don't have much patience for love stories?" She playfully chucked the book in his lap.

He grinned. "You have a boyfriend?"

The braids swung back and forth. "Never have. Just surf buddies. You?"

"Audrey—she's great. Made this scrapbook for me of all my media clippings, gave it to me at the send-off party my parents threw. And she's learned all about surfing—for someone who hasn't ever touched a board, it's impressive. I can't imagine anyone more supportive."

"Sounds like she loves you."

"She does. I just love all these quirky little things about her. It's funny, she keeps a literature list and crosses off the classics as she reads them. Just finished *Moby Dick* and wants me to read it."

"Well, in that case the love story is with a whale. If you're into that kind of thing."

He laughed. "Not for a thousand pages, no."

Heidi uncrossed her legs. Her curvy legs gleamed pure muscle and her otherwise perfect smile revealed a tiny gap between her two front teeth, enough to snare his gaze as she spoke. An undertow of attraction brewed in his gut, and he grew quiet. He slid on his headphones, drowned his thoughts in the Pixies.

Outside the Gold Coast airport, the sponsors' vans awaited Heidi,

SPLITTING THE PEAK / 135

Russell, and a few other pros on the same flight. A ruddy-faced Aussie official in a Quiksilver shirt took the helm. Heidi slid in next to Russell and said, "They treat you a lot better on the CT."

The van cruised for the lineup of high-rise, beachfront hotels, Green Day blaring from the speakers, and all its occupants except for the rep craned their necks for a view of the water; the glistening turquoise awakened Russell from his groggy no-sleep, twenty-four-hours-with-no-shower stupor. The famous right hand Queensland break wasn't firing, the Pacific at Snapper Rocks rolling small, almost flat. As if reading their minds, the rep—an ex-pro from the eighties, his face pock-marked as a reef—piped up at the wheel.

"All everybody talks about from the minute the first southern swell kicks up 'til the day the sponsors pitch their tents is Snapper: are they pumping sand, how's the superbank, what's the story behind the rock, is the break barreling, what about the sand. When she goes off, she's the most gorgeous barrel in the world. Just don't be disappointed if she doesn't. Your sponsors don't want you to be disappointed. We want you to look pretty and party hard, but not so hard you don't win your heats the next day. But you've done your homework, been here before heaps of times, most of you. I'm not telling you anything new. Just reminding you. You'll probably be surfing Kirra and Burleigh Heads, not Snapper, and *you*"—he shot an over-the-shoulder glance at Heidi, the only female riding along—"sheilas will likely be at Duranbah. And who knows? Snapper's always changing shape, never the same for a minute."

Russell and Heidi shared a look. Eyes narrowed, Heidi tossed her head. She leaned over and whispered, "Nice, isn't it?"

"'Sheila,' should I call you that?" Russell joked.

The sponsors' tents were pitched along the beach and the headland above, the banners and flags for Corona, Olympus, and Land Rover flapping; the spectators were fanned out, the sidewalks choked with media and skinny-chested groms, all watching the pros practice. He'd been given the run-down from his sponsors with the publicity schedule: poster signings, a surfing movie premiere, a jet-boat ride with team members, the usual interviews. Already he felt the press of the crowd, voices saying his name as he passed, the cloudless sky and pounding Queensland sun reminding him of Florida and, for a brief moment, Audrey.

*

They had a couple of days before the heats began. The day after next, Russell ran into Heidi at the hotel restaurant. Between sips of coffee she checked out the surf. Her heels propped against the back of the chair opposite, she caught his eye and a moment later was before him with her sloping, tanned thighs, her single, loose braid draped over one shoulder.

"You want to drive down the coast?" she asked. "I could use a day to just kick back and catch waves before the heats start. We could grab a van."

"I've got to get my head straight."

"You need to get out of your head. That's what I do."

"I don't feel like dealing with the sponsors right now. They'll want to send a photographer along."

"So tell them no." His phone vibrated, lit up with AUDREY. She eyed the screen. "Unless you'd rather sit around and read Herman Melville all day."

"I'm not reading Melville," he said. "If you scrounge up a van and find some surf, I'll go."

She smiled. "Roxy'll lend us a van."

As soon as Heidi left, he called Audrey back. Audrey spoke of her college classes and the chilly snap gripping Florida, her voice and the Florida winter as distant as the moon. The sound of her voice only made him want to touch her, to crawl back into the darkness of his hotel room and press his forehead against her bare shoulder.

They drove an hour, caught up to some waves on a cozy inlet not far from Byron Bay, across from a few sleepy surf shops and hippy cafés, pulled off and flashed each other grins. Heidi surveyed the sets rolling in—barely overhead, but fast and clean—just long enough to knot her bathing suit and gather her hair back into a ponytail before charging the water, Russell right behind.

They surfed for three, four hours, no hint of competition between them other than one yelling for the other to go for it when a sizable swell approached, the lineup speckled with a few locals but otherwise not too crowded. Afterward they ducked into a café and underneath a rainbow-strand of Buddhist prayer flags; two sweating Toohey's and quesadillas on the table, they talked surfing: the waves they missed, the waves they got, and the waves caught by the others. By the time they paddled out again the swells had risen from the south, the sets barreling now, a hopeful sign for the resurrection of the break at Snapper Rocks. Russell felt he'd never met a girl so bold and yet so easy to be with as Heidi. He flew down the waves as if the board had melted away from his feet, one hand skimming the glassy inside of the tube, plugged in once again to his Pacific, his mecca.

*

Russell napped and awoke erect, the dreamy remnants of a naked Heidi rocking on top of him still vivid and lingering. He showered and finished before the evening's string of promo parties, envisioning Heidi first, then Audrey in the dim light of his mussed bedroom in Stuart.

The early rounds of competition took place during the day, the officials calling lay-days in between when conditions didn't cooperate. Heidi won heat after heat, advancing steadily towards the finals. Russell hung out in the surfers' tent between events, cheering on Heidi when he wasn't immersed in Graham Greene on his hotel balcony. One day a man, early thirties and slightly built, wound his way through the bustling tent traffic, approached Russell. A press badge swayed against his African-printed button-down shirt.

"Mind if I ask: how would you describe your relationship with Heidi Sierra?" He held up a digital recorder.

The night before Russell and Heidi had hit the casinos and clubs of Surfers Paradise, Heidi in a cocktail dress and heels, her hair blown straight and long, Russell's tucked back into a ponytail. So people were talking.

"We have some good laughs, you know, make fun of the judges we don't like," Russell said. The writer was taking notes. Russell added, "She's like a sister to me." The lie felt thick in his mouth. The writer looked up, nodded, and thanked him.

Russell lost right before the quarterfinals. As soon as he heard the score and knew he was out he took off down the beach, sand scorching his feet—he figured he'd have become immune to the heat by now. A hand gripped his elbow.

"That was some shit they made you guys surf today," Heidi said. She fell into step beside him; one of her braids, still damp, swooped against his upper arm.

"Watch, they'll call a lay-day tomorrow and then that swell's gonna kick up from the south. Watch Snapper go off."

"Then lucky me I guess. Women's quarterfinals are a day after tomorrow."

"I hate surfing crap when you know somewhere on this coast, there's decent surf."

"What are you doing now?"

"No idea."

"I mean, what do you want to do?"

"I don't really feel like talking right now."

"Fair enough, Grumblestilstkin." She lightly slapped his side. His stomach tingled.

The beachfront was clogged with tournament-goers. Two thirteen-year-old fans, a beat-up skateboard underneath each of their arms, approached for autographs. Heidi stood, fist on one hip, said, "Okay, but only if we can borrow these for a couple of hours."

Minutes later, she and Russell hit the street and pedestrian walk, gliding between joggers and hip parents pushing strollers. The breeze blew, salty and clean. Below, the waves crashed at the bottom of the cliffs; the whitecaps erupted and fizzed amongst the rocky tidal pools and lingered in the surf. Skating back, he felt like the rocks were ancient, millions of years old, and something within him felt old, too. When they returned the skateboards, Heidi treated the starstruck owners to giant smoothies, both of them signing autographs before the kids skated off. Alone again, flanked by bare midriffs, faces masked by ice cream cones and frozen lattes, and the dank odor of sunburned flesh and greasy coconut-scented lotion, Russell and Heidi hung back in silence. Dusk was falling. Pop music blasted from the tents along the beach. Heidi hugged him hard; she smelled of the sun and the sea. Then she was gone, weaving in and out of the throng, his arms still suspended with the ghost of her. He had an urge to run, catch up with her at the rocks—and then what? Some kid jostled him, apologized and startled at recognizing him. By the time Russell righted himself, she had disappeared from sight.

When Heidi won the Roxy Pro later that week, Russell was one of the surfers to hoist her overhead and parade her through the crowd, the break a churning cylinder of turquoise glass. Snapper Rocks had roared back to life.

In the frenzy, Russell went several days without calling Audrey and, he was ashamed to admit, had barely thought of her. When he finally did call, he apologized profusely. To his surprise she was more than understanding. "I know everybody parties a lot, after the winners are crowned," she said. "Is everything all right?" Her tone bridled with concern, even suspicion, and he chided himself for his overzealous begging for forgiveness. "Fine, fine, I just miss you is all," he said, and asked her if she was reading anything good lately. "As a matter of fact, I am," she said, brightening. "*The Secret History*." She prattled on about the book, but Russell found it difficult to pay attention. A teammate rapped at his door; Russell was late for the celebratory dinner. He hurriedly changed his shirt, told Audrey they'd have to pick up the discussion later, and hung up. Guilt and a genuine sorrow knotted his gut.

The tour went on several weeks' hiatus. The Quiksilver and Roxy promoters had arranged for their team members to attend the Sydney Opera one night, a black tie affair most of the surfers approached with disinterest and sarcasm; everyone was distracted, preoccupied with reports of the conditions at Bells and their need to increase speed or perfect tricks. Inside the doors, champagne flowed; after two glasses, Heidi slid her arm through Russell's and squeezed his biceps through his dinner jacket; in the cozy haze of the evening, he let her. A photographer from the Sydney paper snapped close-ups of them leaning into one another, grinning madly. The bell sounded and they claimed seats next to one another, their hands centimeters away from touching throughout *La Boheme*.

After the opera the two dozen surfers headed out to a nearby bar. Victoria Bitters and tequila shots were passed around, goofy pranks exchanged, the opera mocked. Heidi hung out with her Roxy teammates while Russell drank and joked with the guys, until he sensed Heidi at his elbow, caught her scent of vanilla. "Some of the girls want to go to a club," she said. She clasped his shoulder and leaned into his ear, adding, "But I'd rather go home with you."

She was pressing against him, her breath tingling his ear and her hair brushing his cheek. Somehow, he heard himself say, "You go ahead. I'm fine."

Minutes later she was climbing into a cab, followed by a South African surfer named Parker Cairns whom Russell particularly disliked for his shallow sarcasm and lack of wit.

The next morning Russell awoke in a hungover fog. It was a warm but overcast summer day, and he thought of heading out to one of Sydney's beaches, Bondi or Bronte, and catching some waves. But whatever energy had been surging through him the last few weeks seemed diminished, blown out. When he pictured going, he saw himself with Heidi and then recalled the night before. He suspected she had hooked up with the South African, and the thought turned his stomach. He picked up his next read, a Salinger book.

Mid-morning, his phone rang. It was her. "Do you have a copy of the *Morning Herald?*" she asked, breathless. "We're on the front page of the Life & Style section."

He fetched the paper from outside his door and shook loose the sections until Life & Style fell out, his face and Heidi's beaming in black and white, her head tilted toward him, her hand cupped to his shoulder in the dress jacket, his mouth open part-way in laughter, glancing toward her. The caption read: "WSL darlings Heidi Sierra and Russell Scott caught looking cozy at the opening night of *La Boheme.*" He hesitated a moment at the "looking cozy" part, hoping Audrey would never see it. He would never be able to explain away the picture; it exposed everything he had been trying to deny. But why couldn't he be in love with two women at the same time? Was it so impossible, so immoral to be with Heidi when Audrey was in college on the other side of the world?

"You want to go for a wave?" he asked. "We don't have many more days off before Bells."

"I'm already going with someone," she said, a splash of disappointment in her voice. "But we'll go again before Bells, no worries."

He thanked her for telling him about the newspaper photo and hung up, unable to shake the loss. He knew, now, that Heidi had gone home with the South African pro when she had wanted to be with him, and he with her. Why had he turned her down? He tucked the newspaper section at the bottom of his suitcase between two magazines. He and Heidi would both be at the next event before and after the ten days of competition. But in a certain way something felt unsalvageable.

At Bells Beach they still watched one another's heats, sometimes grabbed drinks but usually in the company of other competitors or reps, the surfing press tagging along. An ever-growing resentment welled in Russell toward the promo deals, the modeling, and even the charity cricket match he had to play against the national Australian team for publicity. As the winners were crowned—Parker Cairns won Bells—the last parties were thrown and board bags loaded onto airport shuttles bound for exotic points around the globe, Russell felt like he was seven years old again, trying to drop in on a wave when his timing was off and getting pummeled under. Over the phone Audrey's voice sounded more strained, their conversations peppered with more awkward pauses.

"Why won't you be back home until after Tahiti?" she said, breathing hard on her end. "I thought you had some time off after Bells. Can't you fly back for a week?"

One of his sponsor's reps approached after Russell got mouthy with a photographer at a shoot; Russell had been in the freezing water so long he thought he'd get hypothermia even with the wetsuit.

"Better decide what kind of surfer you want to be, mate," the rep said. *Pro surfers never cease to amaze*, he thought. Some of them were the least happy people he knew when they should be stoked to surf as much as they did. Never mind if they had to wake up to a loudmouth called fame.

*

"You heading straight to Tahiti?" Heidi asked Russell outside the hotel, the airport van idling. The waves were peeling slow, midnight blue and crashing white squalls.

"Florida," he said. The wind gusted cold and blew his hair across his eyes, and he tucked it behind both ears. "Changed my ticket. Audrey and I haven't seen each other since January."

Lately all he could think about was sex: his bedroom with Audrey's legs wrapped around him, when he wasn't picturing Heidi. He took in the headland and the rocky coastline across the Great Ocean Road, the darkness of the sea beyond—anything to avoid

Heidi's lips parted in the sunlight, the gap in her teeth, the tan slope of her neck disappearing beneath her sweatshirt.

"Where're you headed?" he asked.

"Some of the girls want to go to Mexico to take a break, but I'll be back in New Smyrna this summer. Maybe head to South Africa from there. Depends on how many photo shoots Roxy wants me to do, you know?"

"Maybe we'll run into each other before Hawaii," he said. A gust lifted Heidi's hair, loose and straight.

"Maybe," she said. They hugged, rocking back and forth a little; she kissed him by the ear before they drew away. Then the rep was slamming the door shut, Heidi's shadow in the tinted window and Russell alone in front of the hotel, hands shoved in his pockets, the van disappearing on the hill, toward Melbourne. He roamed the headland and down to the nearly deserted beach, the dream he'd had the night before resurfacing suddenly, of meeting Heidi at daybreak in one of the semi-hidden coves of craggy rocks, each of them removing their clothes. In the wet sand the surf curled and fizzed beneath them, even though the water was frigid and the April air chilly. Now, with Heidi gone, the aching of the past six weeks turned into an insurmountable, unforeseen grief, as if he'd just woken up and been told he wouldn't be able to surf for the rest of his life. Some possibilities only opened up for so long before they were gone, like Snapper Rocks. The winds and tides changed; sometimes you had to surf the shit.

*

Back home, he struggled to regain his bearings. One afternoon he awoke from a nap in his room. Audrey was propped up on the pillow beside him, naked and writing in her notebook, ankles crossed. "Aren't you finished with that class?" he asked. It was late June. He was leaving again the next morning for Brazil, the Santa Catarina Pro, and didn't want to say goodbye.

"This isn't for class," she said. "It's a story. Fiction."

"What's it about?"

"Two surfers, lifelong best friends who are forced to become rivals in competition," she said. "But they have a deep respect for each other. It ends up happy." She reached up and tousled his hair, kissed his shoulder, light and quick.

"So it's a love story," he said. "About surfing."

"Every surfing story is a love story," she said.

"I guess." He lay back, stared at the ceiling. "Why are you writing about that?"

"To feel what it's like to be you, maybe. Is that okay?" She blushed. Then dropped her pen and cradled his face.

"Sure." He traced her collarbone, could feel himself getting hard. "Why wouldn't it be?"

The next evening Russell was packing his boards when Audrey stormed into the living room, his parents out to dinner and not due back anytime soon. She was clenching the Life & Style section of the *Sydney Morning Herald* which he had stashed between the magazines at the bottom of his suitcase and forgotten.

"Who's this?" she demanded, the pages crackling in her grip. "Don't even try to tell me nothing happened."

"Just some promo event for Quiksilver." He snatched the section from her and smoothed out the page. "That's Heidi Sierra. She won the women's title at Snapper. We're friends."

"You sleep with all your friends?"

"I didn't," he said. He tossed the newspaper and it landed on top of the splayed-open board bag, the room closing in on him. "What were you doing in my suitcase, anyway?"

"You're such an asshole, Russ." She sank onto the couch.

"I love you, Audrey, and I didn't sleep with her—"

"But it looks like you might as well have." She sat there for a moment with a stunned, blank look; he kept rubbing his face, cheeks hot, heartbeat ripping; neither of them moved. Finally she said, "You know what, I believe you, but I can't do this. I really didn't think, with how I know we feel about each other, that the time apart would be this hard. Stupid of me, I guess." She collected her purse and car keys. "Don't you have anything to say?"

"No. I mean, I didn't either. I don't know what to do."

"So go figure out what it is you want to do. Good luck in Brazil." And she left.

Russell stood staring after her at the front door. At last he stooped, picked up the newspaper and tucked it inside his board bag with the t-shirts and towels he used for extra padding. He swore as he packed the boards, his jaw twisting and twitching; tears stung his eyes. He didn't know where exactly he had screwed up, or how, but life sure was blowing out on him.

*

Tournaments came and went. At each stop he scoured the beach and the WSL tents for Heidi, hoping to run into her even if it meant she was on a stop-over with Parker Cairns, the two now a public item. But Russell didn't see her, and guessed he wouldn't until the men's and women's tours reconvened on the North Shore of Oahu with the Triple Crown, four months away. Worse, he missed being able to pick up the phone and talk to Audrey; after the fight, she had insisted on taking a break, that perhaps the long spans apart and intensity of the tour was too much to stay in a committed relationship. For the past year, going on two, she had been there at any hour of the night, from whichever far-flung corner of the globe he might have found himself. In Tahiti, Brazil, and South Africa he emerged with no titles and mediocre performances. His teammates beckoned him to join them for beer and pool, or to catch waves on lay-days, and he made excuses, instead devouring DeLillo, Roth, and Hemingway in his hotel room.

Midsummer, he returned home for a breather and visited his shaper in Cocoa Beach to fine-tune his new board. "That pro you mentioned last time stopped by the other day—Heidi Sierra? Told me to tell you she's back in New Smyrna for a little while, if I happened to see you."

"Did she leave a number or anything?" Russell asked. Heidi had never been one for cell phones.

His shaper ran a hand down the edge of the board as if caressing a woman, shook his head. "But if you ask around, one of the locals'll know how to get a hold of her."

Russell surfed Cocoa until the summer storm struck at two-thirty. Taking refuge at the bar of a beach restaurant, he followed his shaper's advice and got wind of a party brewing up in New Smyrna; a friend of a friend who knew Heidi said she might be there. Russell phoned his parents and told them not to expect him home that night. He headed north, the Beastie Boys blaring and his shorts still damp, tearing along as if some invisible, divine hand pressed against his back. Even after the rains and with the windows down, the wind blew hot, the dash baking, Florida thick in the sweat-rolling soup of July. He could've sealed the Explorer up tight, but he didn't want to—the gusts made him feel alive. He thought of the last time he'd seen Heidi, half a world away with the wind in her yellow hair.

The sun was sinking when Russell pulled up to the bungalow situated a few streets over from the beach, the cracker-style beams of the front porch in need of paint and Heidi's braids a beacon even with her back to him. Surfers, mostly guys Russell recognized from the Junior Pro circuit and a few others he didn't, lolled around, talking and sipping beer; towels and rash guards were draped over the porch rails. From indoors, the air burst with the sounds of the Chili Peppers and the odor of weed. By the time he reached the steps, they were hugging, Heidi laughing in surprise and Russell grinning like a fool.

Heidi rushed out something about she and Russell becoming

good friends in Australia. A tall, skinny surfer with a goatee and the same grey eyes as Heidi's extended a hand, and she introduced him as her older brother, Mack; Russell recognized him as one of the contenders in the Junior Pro from a few years back. Russell had likely surfed against every Junior Pro there at one point, and beat them all. Heidi's scent washed over him as she hovered at his elbow; he was so rattled he could barely speak. "Bells seems so long ago," he said finally. "Heard you won another title."

"I did," she said. "In Brazil." She glanced him over as if trying to determine something. "Where's Audrey?"

"We broke up last month. She gets jealous, I don't know. How about you?"

She forced a laugh, tapped her beer and added, "I'm leaving tomorrow for South Africa to meet Parker. Durban—that's where he's from."

"I know. Not that you were seeing him, but—"

"I'd rather not talk about Parks," she said.

Someone pressed a freezing, slick Corona into his hand, offered shoulder-thumping congratulations at his landing a spot on the Championship Tour that year. Another local held out a Sharpie and an industry mag opened to the wetsuit ad he'd shot on that miserable day after the Bells; on the opposite page was a feature on Heidi's latest win. Russell hastily signed the mag, lowered his voice, and asked, "Is there someplace we can go?"

"Go where?" she said. "I'm staying here overnight. Mack's driving me to the airport in the morning."

"Heidi, please."

"Yeah?" she said, an edge to her voice. She drained the rest of her beer, plunked the bottle on the windowsill and yanked open the door. She called, "Mack, we'll be out back catching up a while."

Heidi led him through a surprisingly neat living room: white cushioned couches and Mexican folk art on the walls, the kitchen counters clean except for the marijuana flecks by the coffee grinder and a few half-empty bottles of tequila and Jack Daniels, out to the bamboo deck. The air was thick with night-blooming jasmine and humidity. They sat down on the couch, their knees bumping and edging apart.

"What are you doing here?" she asked.

"I was getting my board worked on in Cocoa, heard you were back," he said. "I know it's probably weird, me just showing up like this."

"Don't be silly, we're friends. How's the tour going for you?"

"Shitty," he said. "Hectic, really."

"But isn't it incredible to be living what we dreamed up as kids? Sometimes I just can't believe it." She curled her legs up, rested her head back, inches from his.

"I don't know," he said. "In Brazil, right after I lost the heat I got an email from this Hawaiian friend of mine, telling me how great Fiji was and I should hop a plane and come out. And I swear to God, I almost did. I thought, I just lost out surfing crap waves in this tournament, when I could be in Fiji riding perfect, huge sets. My friend was on the tour a few years ago and quit, but he's still sponsored. I figure I could still do pretty well."

"You don't think you'll really quit, though, do you? Give it at least two years."

"If I can hang onto my spot, sure. But I'm not winning like you, superstar." He grinned and pinched her knee.

She poked him back. "What about college? You're the smartest guy I know."

"Maybe. But there are other reasons I want to stay on the pro circuit for now." He ran his fingers down her back, along the strap of her dress.

"Australia was a great time, wasn't it?" she said. "Please don't quit."

"I won't," he said. A second later they were kissing, her body pressing against him and her hands in his hair, his hands gliding under her skirt and up her thighs. From the kitchen came jabs and laughter, the *thunk* of six packs. She edged away from him, straightened out her dress, said, "We ought to go back inside. I don't want to be rude."

"Who cares?"

"Come on," she said, and stood up.

"Wait, will you?" He caught her hand and drew her back. "Don't go tomorrow. I have a few days before I leave for Cali. We can just hang out here and surf. Nobody'll bother us."

She shook her head. "Everybody knows I'm with Parks."

She slipped indoors, and the buzzes of the insects filled the night. He followed, stepping behind the island of six-packs to hide his hard-on. He cracked open a Grolsch over a creased surfing mag, the same copy he'd signed earlier, only this time it was spread open to a shot of Parker Cairns and Heidi, arm-in-arm in Brazil. Despair surged inside him like storm water.

Mack's surfer buddies cornered him throughout the evening, bugging him for stories about the tour. He caved in to their eagerness, but the whole time he kept an eye on Heidi across the room, spilling her own tales in that way of hers he'd come to love—her hands illustrating the air like a hula dancer's. A few girls surfaced, local groupies. Two of them sidled up but he turned his back.

Around midnight everyone left; Heidi and Russell sat diagonal from each other at the table littered with sticky bottles and cups. Russell slouched, toying with a deck of cards. Strands of Heidi's hair hung loose from her braids, and she didn't move to sweep them away from her eyes. Down the hall someone flushed a toilet; Mack emerged and asked Russell if he'd like a pillow or blanket for the couch. Russell muttered something in decline. The door to Mack's bedroom shut, and a Rip Curl poster of a pro in mid-flight over a wave glared back. Heidi stood and gripped the table's edge, her face as pale as a sand dollar. She looked like she might be sick. Russell asked if she was okay. "Fine," she said. She zigzagged to the spare bedroom, and he trailed her. The space contained nothing more than empty, dusty bookshelves, snowboards, and a mattress. He leaned in the doorway, felt like he filled up the whole room, said, "I didn't stay over to sleep on any couch."

She swayed, her eyes pink and watery as she stared at him. She clutched her sides and shook her head. "You're still in love with Audrey."

"No, I'm not," he said quickly, even though he knew this was a lie; Audrey had occupied his thoughts just as much as Heidi since the break-up. But when he backed Heidi onto the bed, she didn't resist but kissed him, dry-mouthed and tasting of tequila. He ripped off his t-shirt and her dress, dropped his shorts; she kicked her underwear to her ankles. A second later he was pounding her fast from behind with all the months of yearning bottled up inside him, Heidi whimpering and moaning. She was really drunk and he knew it, and a voice from somewhere beneath the depths of his own wastedness bemoaned that it wasn't supposed to happen this way, but he didn't care, it was all too late, anyway, wasn't it? And when he flipped her over and continued, she didn't shove him off but let him finish. Afterward, he stalked over to the hallway bathroom and stood in the blast of the shower. He felt simultaneously relieved and devastated. At some point through the pummel of the water, the door clicked, and Heidi's nude, blurry figure knelt at the toilet, throwing up. Afterward, she washed out her mouth and face and left without a word. He waited a few minutes before creeping back to the dark bedroom. He thought of jumping in his truck and flying out of there, the shower having woken him up somewhat, but he sank onto the mattress and Heidi clamped her hand over his, pulling him to her. He burrowed his face in her damp neck until her breathing turned steady and shallow.

In the middle of the night he stirred, pleading in a haze of half-consciousness for her to stay for a few days. "I can't," she murmured. "You know why." She clutched his arm around her and fell back asleep.

The sun spurred him awake. He lay there a little while longer, the garbage truck beeping down the street, the chimes *ching-chinging* in the backyard. The light fell against Heidi's open suitcase strewn with bikinis and the khaki hat she'd always worn in Australia. A minute later, he was in his truck, careening onto the main road, speeding south.

*

Russell tried to wriggle off the thoughts of Heidi which kept bobbing up—her hard body naked underneath him, the way she had wrapped his arm around her in the sheets. Visions of her doing the same with Parks. He wished that they hadn't been drunk, but that it would have unfolded leisurely, like with Audrey. Then August arrived, and he started calling Audrey, who was getting ready to transfer to UF, in Gainesville. But Audrey cut him short, said she didn't want to dish out ultimatums, just didn't think she could handle dating a pro-athlete after all. Reeling, he landed in California and hit the water hard, training for the Trestles, but he scratched out in the first rounds, his worst showing yet and the year almost over. While packing up in his hotel room he grappled with the real probability of his dreams getting sucked down a whirlpool; with the newspaper picture spread over his lap, he tracked down Mack's number, asked him for Heidi's. She had finally caved in and gotten a cell phone. But a voice recording informed him that it was out of range—she could be in Sydney or the Seychelles for all he knew, and she was with Parker, anyway. He tried Audrey, and at her hello he crumpled. "Just wanted to find out what you've been up to lately," he stammered, pacing. "What you've been reading, that sort of thing."

"We said a clean break, Russ. I don't know if this is a good idea."

"I know. But I just read the most amazing book. *The Age of Innocence*. You know it?"

"Sure." Something rustled on her end of the phone. "Haven't

had much time for fiction lately, to tell you the truth. Too much coursework."

"Like what?"

Audrey told him that she'd finally declared history as her major, and had a lot of reading on US literature in the mid-19th century— *Walden* and the like. Thoreau had inspired her to spend more time in nature, so she'd joined the campus Outdoors Club. Their first excursion had been to go freshwater snorkeling at the nearby springs. She had even learned to water-ski and was hoping to wakeboard next. "I've been such a nerd my whole life," she said, a bashfulness to her tone. "It's a big change, but I think I'm actually enjoying it—getting more physical." He could picture her blushing on the other end. The thought flashed through his mind that maybe she was seeing someone else already. His stomach fluttered, and he sank to the floor.

"That's all?" he asked. "I mean, that sounds great. Really terrific. I'm so happy for you, Aud." He hugged his knees to his chest, rubbed his forehead.

"How about you?" she asked softly. "You sound kind of down."

"Oh, the Tour. I'm sure you don't want to hear about that."

"I've got class in forty-five minutes." She paused, rustled papers. "But go ahead."

Relief broke over him, and all of his pent-up frustrations tumbled out. Audrey didn't say much, but when she did her words spoke volumes. She said it must be difficult after a bad heat, not to quit, especially when the reporters barged up. But he was getting to see amazing natural sights. That was an education in itself. Maybe what he needed was to read some Thoreau, gain a more philosophical perspective. She asked how he'd ended up reading *The Age of Innocence*. He'd picked up the novel in a used book shop in South Africa, he said, saw it had won a Pulitzer. The description intrigued him. She admitted she had actually never read it, and hung up.

Two weeks later she called to say she'd taken the book out from the library, and that he was right—it wasn't a chick novel at all, despite the Victorian setting. This time they talked for two hours, Audrey sharing a story about a camping trip with the Outdoors Club that exhausted them both with laughter. "Why don't you come up to Gainesville, next time you're home?" she asked. "Get a taste of campus life."

His coaches weren't happy with his decision—spending his two weeks before the European competitions at the University of Florida, when he should have been hitting the water every day. But as soon as he pulled onto the campus, he felt like he was greeting some other part of himself that he couldn't ignore. He hung out in dorms with Audrey's friends and played hacky-sack on the lawn. He began to see himself with the rest of the kids his age, skateboard clacking beneath him as he wound through crowded sidewalks to class, books tucked underneath his arm. By the end of the visit he and Audrey had reunited as a couple, Heidi Sierra all but forgotten. She had not won another title; from Parker's brief remarks over Kronenbergs in Europe, Russell guessed the two were still together. Russell's own losses pitched him into a precarious position, and he looked ahead to Hawaii with a mixture of excitement and dread. The Triple Crown was his last chance. He would have to fight to keep his spot on next year's tour, if he wanted to be there.

And to his surprise, Audrey wanted to come. At first, he wasn't sure this was a good idea—the press would no doubt hound her on the sidelines, and the fans—but he paid for her ticket anyway. She was scheduled to arrive three days into the Billabong Pipeline Masters, as soon as her semester concluded in December.

In his first week on the North Shore, Russell knew Heidi was at the women's World Cup at Sunset Beach. He had avoided the event altogether, not wanting to run into her with Parker, and yet desperate just for a glimpse. Even after she won—her third title that year, launching her to number two in the world—Russell skirted the trophy ceremony. Just when he thought he might escape a run-in on the day before Audrey was scheduled to arrive, he saw Heidi. At the kick off of the men's heats he spotted her hair, crinkled and cascading down her back, mermaid-like, and the familiar curves of her tanned legs; she stood with Parker under the surfers-only tent, watching with the other pros. Panic jolted through Russell; he hung back at shouting distance but not before Heidi caught his glance, edged closer to Parker. It was the last crushing blow.

Heidi was watching a few days later from the same tent when Russell lost in Round Three—one heat shy of making the Dream Tour two years in a row. But it was Audrey's arms he fell into out of the water and her chest he rested his forehead against, his head and shoulders silent and hidden underneath the towel like a monk, photographers and fans not ten feet away, their chorus of chit-chat and cameras clicking at his back. He let Audrey lead him to the hotel across the road, and when he slammed his board into the sandy yard, cracking it in two and she didn't say anything, he yanked the door shut behind them and told her he was through.

"You'll make it back next year." She threaded her fingers through his hair, and clasped his shoulders.

"I don't want to make it back," he said. "I want to surf, but I need more than that. I need you."

"It was a bad heat, Russ. That's all."

He unwound himself from her grasp. "Is winning so important to you? Because I could care less anymore, I swear."

"I care about us. Even if you keep your sponsors, you'd still have to sell wetsuits. And would that be enough? Without the prestige and money that comes from winning a title?"

He balled up his towel and chucked it to the floor. "You know I'm good enough to keep sponsors hanging around for a long time."

She pressed up against him again, cradled his face in her delicate hands. "If this is what you really want, I'm there for you. Just please think it through. Sometimes we've got to put up with what we don't like, or we lose what we love the most."

Nodding, he hugged her hard. Through the shutters a few rain-drops dotted the broken board.

The next day he and Audrey checked out of the North Shore for Waikiki and a hotel suite overlooking the beach and Diamond Head. His boards remained packed. He spent a long time on the balcony staring at the volcano, thinking about the conversations he needed to have with his sponsors to rework his deals, see how many of them would hang on and for how long once he explained his plans to enroll at college in the fall. The soft, rolling waves of Waikiki reminded him of Snapper Rocks, and the other day, Heidi turning her back as the Banzai Pipeline rose up, the barreling wave stoking the fear he had felt when he first surfed it at sixteen, how he thought he was going to die out there. But as always the ocean washed him ashore, battered and tossed around, and alive; he'd be okay this time if he could stand up and shake off the beating. Audrey was napping; they'd spent the afternoon having sex and talking about what to do next; he'd told her how he would have fallen apart without her there, how much he loved her. He slipped downstairs and bought a ring from one of the shops below. Then he remembered how she had always wanted to go to a real luau, and he booked the dinner show at the Royal Hawaiian.

That night when the dancers pulled Audrey up onto the stage to the surging drumbeats and he proposed, she cried yes.

*

The sponsors, however, were not so happy to hear of his early retire-ment, the contracts not easily negotiable. Russell spent Christmas in Waikiki with Audrey; they had decided to keep their engagement a secret until the buzz about him bailing from the pro-circuit died down, and they didn't plan on getting married until Audrey finished college, at least. But he was scheduled to shoot a surfing blockbuster with six other pros in Bali and had to cut his holidays short; produc-tion started three days before the New Year. He hoped he could keep the sponsorships, surf and shoot for catalogues on his college breaks, and not end up like Heidi's brother, Mack, washed up at twenty-four with nothing to show for all his years in the Grind.

In Bali the sponsors had booked the pros and the camera crews at Nusa Dua in luxury bungalows, an oxymoron Russell inwardly laughed over. Away from the beach crowds and the press, Audrey and Heidi thousands of miles distant, the days ahead were filled with nothing but perfect breaks at Uluwatu and Canggu, tasty satay dishes and temples—the filmmakers wanted footage of the surfers on cultural excursions interspersed with the big airs. So he couldn't have been more shocked to cross the lush courtyard to the breakfast bar one morning and find Heidi with three of her Roxy teammates helping themselves at the tropical fruit platter. His first thought was *What the hell is she here for?* even though his gut told him: you. But neither of them said anything beyond the guise of friendly greetings. Over the clatter of silverware Heidi announced that she'd just taken her first freelance assignment for *Surfer* magazine; while the others congratulated her, he sat silent, wondering where on earth that had come from. He and Heidi sidestepped one another for the rest of the day, the women tagging along to the stuffy tailor shop where the surfers and crewman were outfitted in traditional temple dress, prayer sashes and sarongs required to enter the holy grounds. Nor did they speak at the ritual performance that night given for tourists, dozens of brown-chested men cross-legged and chanting in concentric circles, the *chekka-chekka-chek* of their voices ebbing and rising underneath the moon, even though Russell had claimed the seat next to Heidi and the instant he was next to her, felt the magic snap between them, a wordless completeness he'd only ever known before inside a barrel.

Not until another day passed and New Year's Eve reared up, the guys donning collared shirts over board shorts and the girls in black capris and high heels, everyone roaring off on the backs of mopeds, rattling and honking paper noisemakers all the way to a club in

Kuta Beach, and a couple rounds of tequila shots, did Russell corner Heidi at the bar.

"Sure is funny, you showing up here," he said. "Shouldn't you be training? Snapper's in what, three weeks?"

"Shouldn't you be?" she said. "Besides, how could I pass up a chance to hassle you in person about quitting?" She elbowed him gently, then leaned closer, her hair long and loose.

"There's nothing to hassle about," he said. "All the publicity. I can't stand it."

"Whatever," she said, and flicked her hand dismissively. "You don't have a problem whoring out for the sponsors, selling the dream to all the little groms out there. At least competition's more honest."

"Honest?" he said. He almost spit his beer, thudded the Bin-tang on the counter. "Surfing is supposed to be free of all that bullshit. And we've commercialized it to hell."

"Oh, please," she said. "That's your problem, Russell. You want everything to be easy and beautiful all of the time. Perfect sets." She shoved her beer aside, studied him like she was trying to figure out some unknown break, lips parted, baring the gap in her teeth. "But that's impossible."

"How's Parker?" he asked.

"No idea. I broke up with him in Hawaii." She took a sip of his beer, smiling slightly. "Audrey?"

The dance floor came to a stand-still, chanting the countdown, Prince singing in the background. Russell said, "I'm engaged," and watched her face fall. The club broke out in whistles and wishes for the New Year.

He seized her elbow and steered her out. On the broken sidewalk they caught mopeds back to the hotel, got dropped off outside the gate. The tequila had caught up to him; he needed to grab her to steady himself. They stopped to kiss along the bushes, headlights sweeping over them, now and then coupled with the blast of a horn, but neither of them paid attention. He tripped after her into her

bungalow, spent the night, and woke at dawn with a splitting headache, both of them half-dressed and entangled; he had only one
thought—*What the fuck do I do now?* —and bolted. Lucky for him
the Indian Ocean was flat, the photographers hung over and grip-
ing; the camera crew just filmed the surfers strolling around some
temples; the whole time he thought about Audrey and Heidi. When
he got back that afternoon, he wandered over to Heidi's bungalow.
The door was open; she was barefoot in a Roxy tee and a red sarong,
typing on her laptop. She jumped up.

"About last night," he said. His voice trembled. "Please don't say
anything. Not even to the girls."

"You know, the funniest thing happened on Oahu in December,"
she said slowly. "I ran into that rep who drove us around at Snapper—
you remember the crusty old Aussie? I didn't think he'd remember
me for some reason, but he came right up. He said, 'How are things
with you? How's Russell Scott?' And I looked at him funny, shook
my head. And he said, 'Oh, but aren't you and Russell together?'"
Tears were running down her face. He froze. He had never seen her
like this before, the sassy confidence fallen away. How had it barely
occurred to him that she might feel just as frustrated and upset? She
said, "Don't you want to figure out what it is between us?"

"I can't go back on the tour," he said. "It'll never work. The
pressure killed me."

"I think it's great you're going to college. It's smart." She wiped
her eyes. "None of our bodies last forever. I'm even thinking that
someday, when I'm through with competing and the sponsorships
are done, I'd love to run a surf camp down in Mexico or someplace
like that. No more jet-lag, just teach people to surf on a beach with
a nice break, warm weather. A surfer doesn't need more than two
hundred yards of sand and can live happy forever, if the break's
decent. Wouldn't that be great?"

"That's not going to happen anytime soon," he said. "You're too
good to throw it away."

"No," she said. "I can't quit." Her hand trembled, found the chair and she lowered into it.

The next morning at breakfast, he learned she had packed and gone.

*

With their twenties passed the glory and possibility. Russell and Heidi moved in different yet closely orbiting circles. They surfed reef breaks and barrels, dropping in at Waimea Bay, the deserted stretches of Baja, Soup Bowls, Jaws, Witch's Rock and Salsa Brava, Costa Rica, Cape Hatteras, Puerto Rico, Western Samoa, the wind-swept beaches of Morocco, Malibu and Santa Cruz, Spain and Portugal, the Pipe again and again, the beaches of Sydney and New South Wales and New Zealand, but never did Russell return to Snapper Rocks, nor did Heidi ever win there again.

Russell and Audrey married and moved back to Florida after a brief stint on the West Coast, called home by her father's Parkinson's diagnosis. Audrey worked a county job in archives. She traveled with Russell when she could, reading Victorian novels on the beach; she made it through all of Dickens that way. Russell's deals dried up, one by one, as he tired of the traveling. He found himself with a yearning to return to graduate school, earn his doctorate and teach someplace where he could take off in the afternoons, finished with classes, and catch some decent surf—Hawaii, maybe even Australia or New Zealand. He had some savings and investments from his decade of endorsements and most days, although he dabbled in consulting work, he surfed a three- or four-hour set. He stopped eating meat and fished a couple of times a week, caught his own bait, and sometimes Audrey tagged along.

*

One day in August, ten years after his rookie stint on the WSL tour, Russell opened the email from Heidi. He typed her name in a Google search and her surf camp website popped up. He pored over the whole site and kept the tab open in his browser for days, compelled to look at it now and then, at Heidi's tanned, grinning face peering back, though unsure why. Ten years. He had not seen her since Bali. The website made no mention of it, but she might be married, have kids. One day he returned from the beach, the sets strong and towering from the tropical storm, and banged out a reply, including his mobile number. That evening when Audrey came home, he said he was heading up to Cocoa later in the week; it'd been too long since he'd had some of his round fins worked on at Nielson's, and he wanted to see an old friend who was up visiting there, so he'd probably stay overnight.

"Which old friend?" Audrey asked.

"Just a pro from the tour, retired now," he said, holding his breath. Audrey didn't ask for a name.

He paced during the shaping appointment at Cocoa, and had to keep letting off the gas on the drive up to New Smyrna; Heidi's email directions were printed out and fluttering on the seat next to him, but he recognized the street and the little bungalow of her brother's anyhow. The weather was the same as on the evening of that long-ago summer party: sweat-rolling-off-the-back hot, the stillness of Florida in August relieved by the occasional coastal gust. Someone had smartened up the porch and yard; the house was painted yellow with white trim, the bushes and wandering jew trimmed back, the porch empty except for Heidi in a midnight blue sundress.

They exchanged a brief, polite hug and stepped back, Heidi with a few more freckles dotting her chest and shoulders but otherwise the same curvy legs, Russell's white-blonde hair clipped short, lines around his eyes and mouth when he smiled, too. The same undertow of attraction.

Heidi spoke rapidly, gaze darting, and toyed with the beaded bracelet on her wrist. "Things are going really well with the camp. We just finished our third year. Doesn't compare to the tour, of course, but what does?" She was wearing makeup, he noticed, and her hair was smooth and straight. "What about you?" she asked.

He held up his left hand, fingers stretched wide. "Married. Five years."

"You and Audrey? Congratulations." She said it without a flinch, and her voice contained an extra boost of measured enthusiasm.

They crossed the street to the beach. Russell told Heidi about his hopes for graduate school and relocation to Oahu or Australia, and when Heidi asked if Audrey was up for such a drastic move, he said, "Oh, she loves the idea," omitting Audrey's doubts on purpose, his wife's concern about her father's declining health pitted against his dreams. Heidi wasn't married, had just ended things with a longtime boyfriend two months before. Jogger-couples clipped past the water's edge as the sun lowered, and surfers paddled for the final sets.

"Are you happy?" she asked.

"Yeah," he said, surprising himself by his answer. It was not a lie. "I am."

"I'm glad." She faced him, the sunlight glinting in her still-golden hair, and it took everything in his power not to touch her; if only he could kiss her just once. For the first time since his marriage he felt shackled.

The next moment, Heidi's brother Mack approached them from the water, board underneath one arm and free hand extending to Russell.

At the bungalow Mack's girlfriend joined them, she and Mack smoking cigarette after cigarette, Heidi, Mack and Russell talking about the pro circuit, kids they'd known who had gone on to win titles, but how for every one who'd made it, a dozen or more who'd dropped out or never finished high school, let alone college, or gotten hooked on drugs, ruined by money and fame, and parents hungry for both. "You have any kids?" Mack asked Russell, who was sitting next to Heidi a good foot apart on the couch, though the invisible snap of magic between them was stronger than ever. Russell could feel himself redden; he drew up on knee and laughed nervously. He said, "We're not sure if we want any." Heidi said something encouraging—maybe once he and Audrey moved, the timing would be right, but he didn't reply. He and Audrey had only grown more bookish and insular, and despite dropping in on the occasional yoga class, Audrey remained skeptical of her body, even fearful. He was certain if he'd been with Heidi, having children would not have been a question.

To change the subject, Russell commented on how nice the bungalow looked—framed surfing posters of Heidi lined the hallway; when he glanced by on a trip to the bathroom, the guest quarters looked like a boutique hotel suite with teak furniture, a matching comforter and curtains. "Heidi's done that for us," Mack said quietly, and Heidi's gaze dropped to her lap. "Gotta put all those winnings somewhere," she said. "And it was silly for him to keep paying a mortgage when I was crashing in the spare room for so long, anyway."

Throughout dinner, the skies poured. The four of them dined at a Greek restaurant in town; Heidi and Russell ordered the same thing: fresh snapper which turned out to be as big as board fins. Russell scraped the scales from hers, then his, while Heidi laughed, joking that it was payback for all those times on the tour when she'd taken care of his drunk ass, him laughing and unable to deny it. How could it be that so much time could pass like nothing at all, and two people could pick up as easily as they had left off, finishing the ends of each other's sentences, and when their time together had really only amounted to a few distilled months on the other side of the world? On the way back they made a pit stop for beers, Heidi and Mack's girlfriend remaining in the SUV while Mack and Russell ducked into the convenience store. "Sure can tell you two were good friends," Mack said. The words stuck like sand but Russell didn't say anything, too hung up on the past tense.

Back at the bungalow they drank beers and talked: Heidi about

San Juan del Sur and her camp, which catered exclusively to women; Russell about his newfound passion for fishing. The time crept close to midnight. Mack's girlfriend said goodnight and disappeared into the bedroom; she had to get up early for work. Mack smoked half a joint and followed soon after. Heidi and Russell moved out to the back porch. They faced each other at the bistro table, a few feet from where they'd first kissed a decade before, the air once again heavy with the scent of jasmine and the moon at Heidi's back, high over the glimmering ocean.

Russell's knee jounced beneath the table. "You look really great," he said at last.

"Thank you, Russell." She had always called him that: *Russell*, never *Russ* like everybody else. She'd said the words faintly, her manner so much more subdued than how he remembered her at twenty. Maybe even with sadness.

"Kind of funny, getting your email the other day and now we're sitting here. After so long. I mean, I don't keep in touch with any of the guys from the tour. I'm sure you still do."

"Not really."

"No? What about Parker Cairns?"

She scoffed, shook her head. "God, no. I've found my own little corner of the world. And I guess I don't care to know about anyone else, except for you. Which might sound strange."

"Not really," he said, voice wavering. "When I think back to that year—even the years leading up to it, somehow—all I can think of is you. Even though we never really got together."

"Why didn't we?"

"The timing was never right, I guess." He sat rigid, the wrought-iron digging in. "God, I didn't think tonight would be this intense." He forced a laugh. A long silence passed, beers empty but neither rising to fetch replacements.

"It always was like this, at least for me," she said finally. "From the minute we started talking on the plane, remember? I've always wondered what you felt for me—if it was like what I was feeling for you."

He stared at his feet. "I was just so immature then. I really blew it."

"But so did I," she blurted. "I was in love with you, in Australia. You drove me so crazy, every time we hung out. I wanted to be with you so badly, and it was such torture. But I waited and waited. And finally, I just couldn't take it anymore. When the night at the opera rolled around, I told myself, this is going to be it, I'm going to find a way to go home with Russell if it kills me. And I don't know what happened, we split off, I gave up and went off with Parks, who I didn't even *like*." She slumped, hugging her chest. "So we both screwed it up."

He thought of Audrey back home, reading in bed with her book light, the dog at her feet. "I'm so sorry," he said. "And I don't live my life with many regrets, either, but one thing I will regret for the rest of my life is not pursuing you in Australia." As soon as he said it, he felt like the world's biggest asshole.

"What do we do?" Heidi's tone was pleading; grief bit the air. "I guessed you might be married, or with someone, at least. It's naïve to not think otherwise, at our age. But I've never felt this"—she gestured between them—"with anyone else. Have you?"

He hung his head. "I don't want to be selfish," he said. "I don't want to hurt anyone." When he looked up he forced himself to stare beyond her, at the moon overhead, the steel grey waves peeling. Anything but jumping up and embracing her.

"I'm not going to ask you for anything," she said. "I'm single. I've got nothing holding me back. But you." Her voice trailed off. "I'll be here another couple of weeks."

"I'd like to see you again," he said quietly.

"It's up to you." She gathered the beers. "God, it's late. You driving back tonight?"

He startled, remembered that he'd told Audrey not to expect him back until the next day, leaving the gap open for Heidi. A fantasy. But now he panicked at the sudden weight of it all crashing down on him, sucking him under. He needed time to think. He arose, felt in his pocket for his keys. "I'll call you," he stammered. "But we've got to be careful."

What was he doing? He loved Audrey, but here was Heidi who he loved, too—because what else could it be? What else besides love could reemerge through space and time and remain so unchanged, spin them on end and make him remember what it was to be young again? Was lust capable of doing that, the connection merely preserved by youthful memories? He didn't think so. Heidi walked him to his truck. They stopped underneath the streetlight, the breath of the ocean in the distance. He entwined his hand in hers, squeezed it. Her lip quivered; he thought he might cry, too, if he wasn't so overjoyed to be so close to her. "Maybe the best thing is for me to take a surf trip to Nica for a week," he said. "I'll see you soon, okay?"

"We'll always be friends, won't we?" she said. "Even when we're seventy years old." She was squeezing his hand back, hard; they swayed with their hands clasped like children. He pulled her into a long hug, rubbing her back; she kissed him lightly on the shoulder before he climbed in the truck. He hadn't reached the end of the block and the tears were pouring; at the stoplights he lifted his shirt to dry his face. Before he turned onto the highway he had to pull over, but the pain was worse than ever and didn't subside with the tears, even when he had beat into his brain that they had both screwed it up, and he could never see her again.

When he reached Stuart, Russell rolled past his driveway and out to the beach; he didn't want to face Audrey until he could sort out his head and heart. Could it be possible for him to fly down to Nicaragua, just once, spend a week with Heidi, no harm done? He still shot footage for sponsors sometimes; Audrey wouldn't question it. He pictured himself packing his boards for any other surfing business trip, he and Heidi on some isolated cove of Nicaragua's southern coast. No one would ever find out, and she wouldn't say anything. But one thing he couldn't bear to have happen was to devastate Heidi even more. He sat in the sand until sun up. The first locals paddled out, the gulls swooping and crying overhead. A couple and their dog appeared at the far end of the beach, figures like black sticks. The dog dashed into the surf. Every so often, the man's whistle carried sharp on the breeze. The couple walked and took turns throwing a ball to the dog, and in between throws they held hands. Was he really going to ruin his marriage for a memory? Because he was happy with Audrey; he had no doubt. The feelings he and Heidi shared of that time—those were powerfully real, a connection that would remain. But they had both changed in subtle, significant ways, and trying to recapture whatever they'd had now, he sensed, would be in vain, a misguided fantasy that would only cause anguish. After a while, once he was certain Audrey had left for work, he crawled home and into bed.

*

After the lights of Russell's truck disappeared from sight and Heidi retreated to the guest room of her brother's bungalow, she tugged her old paperback, *The Dogs of Winter*, from her suitcase and from between the covers slid out the newspaper clipping of her and Russell the night of the Sydney Opera, its edges wilted and frayed. She hugged herself and cried quietly for a while, her tears dropping onto the newsprint. What she yearned for she couldn't remember exactly. As the years passed, her memories of those days in Australia blended together—of skateboarding behind Russell above Snapper Rocks, ducking into pubs and grabbing beers after heats. The beach at Surfers Paradise at night, the din of some sponsor's party and techno beats at their backs as they talked and brushed elbows in the cool sand. What washed up with the passage of time and soaked in more acutely was a feeling, a mixture of joy, freedom and abundance, and a childlike ease. Some nights, in her beach house overlooking

San Juan del Sur, she had awakened with her eyes damp and wandered over to gaze at the dark shadow of the Pacific. She wondered if Russell ever thought of her, if in some parallel universe she would slip inside and find him sleeping next to her empty, restless place.

So he'd felt the same during that year on the tour—what did it matter? He was married. Whatever they had shared belonged to that time, and couldn't exist now, not in the same way. She shoved away the clipping, opened another beer. Turning on the TV she found a reality show, something mind-numbing about models but the tropical beach looked familiar, anyway. After a couple of minutes, she lost interest, picked up a tattered *Sports Illustrated* and paged through absently. Her brother had left half a joint in the ashtray. She lit the stub and settled back on the couch.

EXALTED WARRIOR

The sessions started in June. The young woman would pull up behind the warehouse, enter through the unmarked door—green. The room always the same. No A/C, just ancient fans. First the luminescent screen. The old man showed her images, examples. Digital photos of other women. On mattresses, half-nude. On ladders, sometimes, or stairs. Sometimes she brought scarves, jewelry. He liked gauzy skirts. In the bathroom she undressed. Brown-ringed toilet, no paper. Never any soap. She always felt watched there. Final talk to the mirror.

She was keeping the tradition alive. They, the two of them. It might die without her. If they weren't discovered first.

He'd drag out the mattress. Or a chair, lamp-lit. She arranged herself. As discussed, unless she forgot. He adjusted her limbs, chin. Treated her like open flames. Or a glass figurine. Like she might scream. But she couldn't afford to. He could do anything.

Sometimes he used electrical tape. Marked feet, shoulders, the sheets. She froze in place. The first ten minutes killed. Quiet torture, until the mind settled down. Accepted. Once that happened, no problem. She could last. Twenty, thirty minutes, no break. Until her skin got hot spots from pressing for so long onto the back of the chair or arm rests. Then up to shake out. Bathroom, water, but not too much. They aimed for three hours. The lamps were bright and blazing. Could melt makeup. She never wore any. Sometimes he played music, jazz or hippy anthems from long ago. Often he preferred silence. Occasionally they talked. She only knew him by surname. Rafkin.

She was Tasha. Not her real name.

*

On the night the Shadowmen patrol swept through and Liam disappeared, Tasha had been in the warehouse with Rafkin, who had handed her a pair of gold sandals, told her to put them on and nothing else. From the main street the patrol cars first declared their warnings in the pitched tones of Mandarin, which sent a shiver to her stomach like getting a paper cut, before repeating themselves in a buttery, even, Anglo-male voice: "You are in a Red Zone. Your cooperation is essential to everyone's safety. Be on the lookout and report any suspicious activity. The Internal Enemy is often next door."

Rafkin said, "Let's have some Vivaldi," and the notes drowned out the loop.

"Who's this one for?" Tasha asked, her lips stiff, expressionless.

"A new client," he replied. Rafkin ran a thumb through his straight white hair, adjusted his glasses. He might have been a scientist, one of the mentors from Liam's team. "Somewhere in Beijing. At least I think that's the address. I haven't bothered to translate it. How's your Mandarin?"

"Okay," she said, meaning shitty. Russian was becoming more useful these days. "Doesn't it bother you, not knowing who they're for?"

"Not really," he said, "if I know it's not my idea from the beginning. The sandals, for instance—too gimmicky for my taste. But none of them are mine anyway. When you're the creator of something, you're a servant. The work passes through you."

"How do you know it's not a sting?"

"Why ruin the moment with a thought like that?"

"So you don't know."

"It used to be said that working for the universities was safe." He chuckled. "But what is safe? This one, he came through a very reliable source. So don't let your worry seep into the picture."

"I just like to be cautious."

"Where it ends up—why is that such a concern to you?"

"I don't know," she said. And it was true. Rafkin's style was like Monet's; most of the time the image on canvas barely resembled her likeness. Maybe she just enjoyed the feeling of taking part in a beautiful, uncommon thing. Or the quick barter—she was part of the underground now, not just thinking, but doing. Like Liam.

Rafkin scratched his face and stepped back, regarding his work. His mouth parted, revealing the gap between his graying front teeth. "Nothing is safe," he said. "That's the only truth."

*

Her real name was Laura. Soon after they'd met, Liam convinced her to use an alternate for any situations where she wouldn't want to be traced if she was ever questioned by Shadowmen . She didn't know Liam's real name. One of the technologies he had developed was a program which interrupted the syncing of personal devices, like MiniSlates, with the Internet, supplanting the user's identity with a false one. He claimed he had been with the Second Resistance for so long the young man with the other name had died.

That night, after Rafkin had paid her (tomatoes from his hanging plants, eggs, and honey—a rare find) she rode north across the city, pleased with her earnings and eager to show Liam. Her boyfriend didn't like her modeling, didn't trust Rafkin even though she'd met the artist through one of Liam's underground connections. "That guy could have cameras everywhere, be turning in pictures of you posing naked to the Morality Watch, who knows?" Liam would say. "Or what if his little operation is busted while you're there?"

Rafkin was nobody to worry about, she'd assured Liam. The old man was a harmless former professor, passionate about art. Rafkin had survived the Purge and an internment at the Ivory Tower, plus had an elite group of clients who protected him. What she didn't admit to Liam was how she never felt completely at ease in the warehouse. She didn't feel like Rafkin would try to grope her at some unsuspecting moment or even that a patrol might bust down the door. More like a slight, nagging sense that she would come to regret having posed for him. In the meantime, she and Liam needed to eat, and the barter was good—each session worth two bags of groceries, if she had no money in her account, which she never did. Since leaving school she had a block on her number which ensured any official income she earned went to the government first. Her profile might read as Tasha, but her number remained the same.

Several times at intersections her old car baulked and repeatedly announced a wrong location. She leaned forward, tomatoes sliding from her lap, and thumped the dash.

"Home," she said, and again, louder.

The last mechanic she'd visited had warned her that she desperately needed a new vehicle; the computer was so old he could hardly find parts for it any more—one of the first fully autonomous models that had been bought up by the rideshare fleets almost immediately after their release. Hers would have belonged to someone wealthy, a good cover. With any luck she appeared like an elderly Gen X lady reluctant to give up her private ride.

"Recalculating," the car chirped.

She settled back, gathered the tomatoes, cool and smooth, scented with earth. Later, when she sliced them open, seeds would spill out, the taste sharp and full-bodied. Forgotten. Tomatoes, the real kind with seeds inside that you could replant and grow, could get you in a lot of trouble.

Trouble was the first thing that entered her mind when the car turned into her housing complex. The darkened units, solar panels ripped up and tossed in the lawns, the dumpster and recycling bins burning in the lot, the door to their unit open and light flooding out—Shadowmen had come.

She approached slowly, dropped the bag of groceries inside the porch. From an upstairs unit she heard muffled sobbing, a shriek. Down the walkway the fluorescent bulbs were still lit, albeit dim, probably running on generator life. From the shrubbery a pair of legs jutted out—hairy and male, streaked with blood. Actual authorities wouldn't be more than a few hours away, a day or two or if their complex was lucky. She didn't approach the body.

She used the flashlight feature on her MiniSlate as she entered. The kitchen cabinets and fridge had been ransacked, the pantry she and Liam had worked so hard to stock over the year empty. The unit would be written up and, in the very least, interrogated and fined for having a contraband food supply. She knew what penalties the violation entailed: a hefty fine she wouldn't be able to pay, so community "care" work in lieu. Her breathing turned shallow, jagged. Around the corner and all the electronics were absent from their docking stations, of course. Thank God she used her MiniSlate and its false ID now for everything. The cushions had been yanked from the couches, the bathroom toiletries spilled over the sink. She braced herself for blood, the shadow of Liam's body hanging or lying in the bedroom. She crept down the hall, her voice a husky, aching whisper, saying his name, straining to catch a groan, not wanting to find the worst. But nothing.

She hovered halfway between the closet and the bed, trying to recall what Liam had told her to do if he were ever disappeared, as they called it, by Shadowmen. When she was a child, she remembered her father explaining how they were never to speak publicly bad opinions about the government, because someone who heard you could call you a terrorist for saying those things—that you were anti-American, unpatriotic. You would be returning from school or the stores; a van would drive up, military-looking men would jump out, grab you, and whisk you away. You would be labeled a terrorist—an "Internal Enemy," as the Chinese liked to call it—and because of this they could lock you away forever, never tell your family where you were, or even if you were alive. Only in recent years, with the U.S. government's dire fiscal situation, had the authorities turned to posting hefty bonds for I.E.s they considered valuable. Families who had the means, or were desperate enough, could pay the bonds in exchange for a release and trial date; this guaranteed nothing more than knowing a loved one was alive, and a slim chance at freedom.

"Techs are especially valuable to the Chinese," Liam had told her on more than one occasion, usually one of their late-night talks. "And especially brilliant tech geeks, so they wouldn't likely kill me. At least not right away."

"But what if it's the Shadowmen who come for you?" Tasha had asked. "How are they to know you're a brilliant young anything, except an anti-government radical?"

"We'd just have to wait it out," he replied. "If there's a bond, they'll make that known pretty fast. It won't be easy. But if they take me when you're not around, just stay put for a couple of days. You've got to gather information before you make any moves to reach out. Or for the people I know to find you."

Now she pictured him drugged, gagged, in a van speeding south on one of the city highways. "Don't worry, Liam," she said to herself, curling up on the mussed sheets, pressing her head to the pillow as a rush of tears wet her vision. "I'll save you."

*

The next morning, she sat inside Rafkin's warehouse studio, sunlight streaming in the high slatted windows. Rafkin offered what legally passed for coffee—a substitute made from carob. "No jolt in that, I'm afraid," he apologized, handing her the cup. "But you've probably had enough jolts for a while."

"What do I do now?" she said, cradling the cup. She wasn't used to the warehouse in the daytime. The dusty pictures leaned from the walls; Rafkin's breakfast dishes were piled next to the sink. She had been up most of the night, putting the apartment back in order, wondering if she should attempt to contact Liam's friends. When she awoke the only person she thought to seek out was the painter. She asked, "Where do you think they've taken him?"

"Maybe the Federal building, or even Thirty-third Street," Rafkin replied, meaning the old county jail. "You might consider waiting until they come to you. They're hoping you'll panic."

"I am panicked," she said. "When they come around, you know what they're going to ask. 'Why aren't you working? How are you feeding yourself? Who pays these bills?' What am I going to tell them?"

"You came home and the food was there," he said "Maybe someone left it at your doorstep, and your boyfriend stocked the pantry. How are you supposed to know what's organic or not? Are you a scientist?"

She smiled. "I can always show them my progress reports." Despite her best efforts, she had never risen above average in any class, math or science. Ever since she could remember, school had been a struggle, like her brain was swimming upstream. She had always envied people like Liam, a material science genius plucked out of school at sixteen to attend the Zucker-Gates Institute. The best she could hope for was a coding job someplace.

"No, that won't work." Rafkin sipped with a vacant stare, lost in thought. "What you need is an injection of money. Two or three million, at least."

"You think the fine will be that much?"

"Not the fine. Liam's bond."

"A bond's not going to exist if they've decided he's to disappear. Everything is in the computers and devices they took."

Rafkin shook his head. "There's not a Second Resistance cell today that's not keeping some information strictly word-of-mouth." He nodded toward an oil painting on the wall by the bathroom of a curvy brunette woman sprawled on a bed, rosebud lips parted.

"One of my ancestors, before she was caught for hiding intellectual subversives in Europe. They dragged her body through the streets."

She'd always liked that painting whenever she passed it on her way to undress, the liquid look in the woman's blue-green eyes. "Did you paint it from a photo or imagination?"

"It's her self-portrait. It was hidden and passed down after her death."

"It's stunning," she said. "You really can't help me?"

"I barely squeak by after the clients take their protection fees, the landlord his cut. And I have the others, you know. My little brood."

"I need more than a bag of groceries anyway."

He leaned across the greasy table. "There are things you can do," he said. "I hate to mention them, but—"

"Don't," she said. "I know."

"Okay then," he said, rubbing his forehead. "Okay. Then take care of it today." He sighed. "They'll be coming."

She nodded, rising.

*

She and Liam had talked about her donating before but had always promised one another that it would remain a last resort, "if things get life-or-death bad," as he'd said. Liam had gone to the clinics and given blood and semen for money regularly for a while; how many little Liams might be running around in the world, here or in Europe or China, was the running joke. Both had been zero-risk decisions, the procedures harmless. And they had always promised to make the decision together. *Oh well, here we are*, she thought, the car pulling into a spot outside the address she had programmed from the warehouse. The computer had brought them out of the Red Zone, closer to the resorts and theme parks. The solar panels on the glass-planed skyscraper tilted toward the sun like houseplants. The suite was on the thirty-first floor, and she winced upon entering the corridor. EGGSELENT ALTERNATIVES! read the brass name plate, with the smiley-faced egg engraved as part of the logo. *A chicken egg—how absurdly stupid*, she thought.

The doors swept shut behind her, and she found herself in another corridor, dimly lit. Her MiniSlate chimed, the case damp in her palm. "Checking in to Eggselent Alternatives," the screen read. "Welcome." On either side, hologram posters swirled to life. Her airbrushed face in cap and gown beamed back from the wall, and a silky woman's voice said, "As a recent grad, you're eligible for our Fast Track Tuition Reimbursement Plan. Ask your broker for more details." She descended the hall, the posters on either side flashing to life and addressing her by name as she passed each one. One depicted a photo of her and her friend Alexia laughing at an underground party—*If only they knew*, she thought, smiling to herself—the voice saying, "Refer a friend, and you both receive a bonus upon completion of cycle retrieval." Still other holograms inserted her image into imaginary scenarios: Tasha next to an Asian couple on a couch, the man bouncing a chubby baby on his knee ("Discover the ultimate joy. Give a loving couple the gift of life"); Tasha shaking hands with a man in a lab coat, surrounded by beakers, test tubes and slides ("As a Donor Angel you'll be at the front lines of science, contributing to the future of humankind"). The voices faded behind her as she entered an empty seating area.

Her MiniSlate chimed again. "Registration and prescreening," it read. "Gathering medical records. Gathering family history. Infectious disease screening. Please step over to the sink at the corner station." She followed the instructions, washing her hands with antibacterial soap and placing her right index finger in a small padded vice. After the pinprick, a test strip gathered the drop of blood. Her MiniSlate read, "Updating. You are clear of infectious diseases. Registration complete. Congratulations, Tasha. You are pre-approved. Wait here and a broker will meet you shortly."

No going back now. She sat on a couch, wondering if the broker would appear in hologram form or as an actual human being; live interactions were rare these days. Holograms were frustrating, but people were too. At least a hologram was just delivering its pro-grammed speech, the interaction relegated to whatever information was on your mobile device. A person could look right at you and lie, or be trained to pick up your body language and verbal tics. How would Liam advise her to proceed? The thought of Liam in an interrogation room somewhere, bloody and bruised, made her light-headed and queasy. The bond, when would they announce it? Earlier she'd searched the usual government websites announcing the latest IEs and their corresponding bonds, but nothing yet. *You better be alive, dammit*, she thought. Maybe donating wouldn't be so bad, the stories which rippled through the underground and posted at back-door discussion forums only half-true. Maybe she'd be one of the strong ones, and emerge intact.

Doors slid open. A middle-aged blonde woman, lab coat over her silky blouse and skirt, approached. Her eyes were deeply set behind a small, perky nose. She introduced herself as Alice, the broker. "We just have one more set of tests to run before I walk you through the facility," she said. "I'll design your forms and contract, get you in the system and matched with a recipient as soon as possible. I don't know if you're aware, but you have a very desirable gene pool. You should have seen me back there as your information was streaming in. I could hardly wait to meet you."

"What makes my genes so desirable?" Tasha asked.

"You've got traces of some of the top-requested rare lineages: Jewish and Japanese," Alice said. "Are you aware? Those can be worth a lot of money."

They stepped from the waiting room into a brightly lit corridor that looked like a hospital wing. Employees in scrubs—nurses, Tasha assumed—hurried between rooms, electronic pens flying over their MiniSlates. Along the huge windows a dozen young women around Tasha's age appeared to be waiting. Some slurped iced stimulant drinks while others stared off vacantly; Tasha could hear the music blasting from their ear buds as Alice escorted her past. A MiniSlate buzzed, and one of the prospective patients stood up and slipped into an examination room, someone in a surgical mask greeting her at the door.

Alice ushered Tasha into an examination room. Tasha was given a quick pelvic exam and ultrasound of her reproductive organs by a nurse, then was led to another room marked REGISTRATION where Alice greeted her from behind a desk, a hologram presentation pre-loaded.

"How did it go?" Tasha asked, taking a seat. "Did I pass?"

"We'll know in just a few minutes," Alice said. "By the time we're finished with the Cycle Summary overview."

The hologram presentation followed, with a hologram Alice as host who welcomed the prospective Donor Angel, an unnerving juxtaposition with the real Alice sitting nearby and nodding as the overview ensued. "We are a brand-new multibillion dollar facility—the first in Florida to handle all testing, patient monitoring, retrieval and research under one roof," her image declared proudly, the hologram slightly drifting into blizzard. The overview highlighted the steps of a single donation cycle. Each cycle took several weeks. Once the Donor Angel was matched with a client, she took birth control pills for ten days, followed by a series of self-administered injections which stopped her menstrual cycle, followed by another ten days of fertility hormone injections. Usually the process matured eight to fifteen eggs which were then aspirated vaginally by a doctor, with the Angel under something called "Twilight Sedation." The entire harvesting took only twenty minutes, after which the Donor Angel could go home, rest, and begin the entire process again if she hadn't reached the peak age of thirty-two. Hologram Alice reappeared to conclude the orientation: "It is a wonderful feeling to know you have the honor of helping a couple achieve their dream, or a scientist his breakthrough. Welcome to the Donor Angel team." Program over, the hologram vanished. Tasha faced the live Alice, who sat erect and beaming.

"The overview didn't mention anything about risks," Tasha said.

Alice beamed wider, the creases of her deep-set eyes crinkling. "There is a small chance of the ovaries becoming overstimulated by the hormones," she said. "Usually it's nothing more than some swelling and discomfort. The majority of our Angels come through just fine. In fact, most donate again and again."

"What about in the long-term?"

"Again, we really can't prove any definitive links," Alice said, shrugging, still smiling. "Shall we get started?" She brought up an e-form on the glass table between them, the fine print all but legible in the brilliant illuminated green.

"Wait. How much is the compensation?"

"Well, that depends on your credentials and pre-screening results, doesn't it?" Alice brought up another form alongside. "Looks like your ultrasound was perfect. Let's have a look at your profile." She brought up another screen, Tasha's full history mapped out before them. Alice's perky nose twitched as she studied the data. "Too bad your grades were so average, but a state university isn't the worst place. Not Ivy League, mind you. Your height, weight and symmetry are all ideal. Were you interested in our Fast-Track Reimbursement Plan?"

"Maybe," Tasha said. "What's that?"

Alice spoke quickly, and her gaze didn't leave the forms she was modifying. "The Fast-Track signs you on for a minimum of three Donor Cycles, with an advance payment today. As soon as you create a username and password, you're registered on our website as a Donor Angel. The monetary advance lifts any hold on your citizen account and alerts the government or any employers of your enrollment. Moreover, it gives you protected status, just like military personnel." Alice looked at her. "What do you think?"

"The advance is how much?"

"Your payment for each cycle would be two million dollars," Alice said. "The Fast-Track Plan pays you half up front for all three.

So you could leave here with three million, minus our fifteen-percent brokerage fee, and your account will be clear today."

Three million minus fifteen percent wouldn't be enough, Tasha thought. But it was a start. She picked up the electronic pen and her signature poured out, a liquid emerald green. Later she would go online and see what kind of hard information she could find about donating multiple times, how she might protect herself.

Before leaving, Alice brought up the registration screen and selected an attractive headshot from Tasha's MiniSlate album for the Donor Angel website. Alice also told her to create an alias. "All your information is kept strictly confidential with us," Alice said. "That's what the brokerage fee ensures: that the scientists and couples who are searching for matches will never know your true identity, just the name on screen. Can't ever have too much protection." Tasha hesitated and selected Muse2017. Password: Miracle. It would take just that for her and Liam to make it back to one another alive, unscathed.

*

By the time she reached the parking lot, her MiniSlate had finished updating. During the forty-minute drive home she surfed through her entire profile. Eggselent Alternatives! was now listed under Employer. Among other things, her e-passport, purchasing rights and bank account had been reinstated, the latter still showing the amount of just over two and a half million dollars in transfer. When the engine choked off the I-4 exit ramp, she thought, momentarily, *I could get a new car this week.* But every cent of this had to go for Liam. If she hadn't gotten involved with Liam and his group in the first place, she wouldn't be doing this, but then again, where would she have made it this far without him? She could hear her father's voice saying how disappointed she'd made him for doing such a thing, but she didn't think so, and her father wasn't around anyway. You could always be worse off; she might have been born in Latin America, or Africa, or the Philippines, a woman whose genes weren't wanted, whose only option was to be a surrogate countless times, to give up on having her own children until, after a lifetime of birthing babies for wealthy strangers, she'd face an early and forgettable death.

Her call pulled into the lot. In front of her building two white government-style SUVs with black windows glinted in the subtropical sun. She had known Rafkin would be right; they'd be waiting to speak with her, might even bring her in for interrogation. But her knees still went watery at the sight of the two men in white suits and sunglasses on her porch. Breathe. Follow the breath. Stay centered. Like she'd learned from that underground friend of Rafkin's, the yoga lady—Marilyn. "Tell the truth, but make it your truth because they can tell when you're lying," Liam had told her. She approached the porch, felt for the MiniSlate in her purse. "May I help you?" she asked.

One of the agents leaned against the doorway, the outline of his muscled physique flexing underneath the white suit. He addressed her in Mandarin. "Your unit raises some questions," he said. "We're hoping you'll be able to clear up what your companion has left in the dark." So Liam had been turned over to the authorities.

"I don't know," she said, her Mandarin slow. "I don't speak Chinese well."

"English, then," the other agent said, stepping forward. He was taller, his head slightly too small for his long frame. "Neither of you seem to be working. Please explain."

"Liam works," she said, shrugging. "Every day. Top secret project, is all he says. He doesn't give details."

"He's not listed on any government projects," the first agent said. "His name isn't registered with the corporations, either. But we're not telling you anything new, now are we?"

"He was hired right out of the institute, as far as I know," she answered.

"And he never mentions who he's working for, or the names of anyone else on the project?" The first agent stepped closer, frowning.

Even his facial features struck her as muscular. "You never looked through his profile, just for fun? Saw his name wasn't really Liam Fisher?" He reached over and removed her sunglasses, the cool sleeve of his suit brushing her hot arm. A dry breeze stirred the air; the summer had been plagued by drought. Her throat was dry too, and she swallowed.

"What about all the organics we uncovered here last night?" the other agent said. "If neither of you are working legally, those are contraband."

"I am working," she said. She fished out her MiniSlate, handed it over. "Look."

The taller, gawky agent's gloved finger skipped along the screen, raised an eyebrow. "A Donor Angel," he said. "Just registered today. A little sudden, no?" He and the other agent exchanged glances. Her MiniSlate chimed; the agents handed it to her.

"A message from my broker," she read aloud. "She's found a match. I'm to login tomorrow morning and start the process."

The shorter agent's nostrils flared. "I wonder how your boyfriend might take the news," he said. "About you becoming a Donor Angel."

"He won't have to wonder for long," she said. "I'll be posting his bond shortly."

The agents started to leave. The tall one reached above his head for the hanging plant, spun the base. Flecks of dirt fell. "What pretty flowers," he said. "Doing your part for the atmosphere, I see. You like to garden?"

"Not me," she replied. "I can't keep anything alive."

"Let's hope you're more useful than your boyfriend," he said. "Angel." He let the door bang behind him as the SUV started up. The men climbed inside and sped away.

*

Nightfall, and the hum of an approaching drone and thud of a package on her doorstep. For the rest of the afternoon she'd scrolled through secret groups and forums, reading the firsthand accounts of those who'd donated before her. The mainstream media spin had been overwhelmingly positive, of course, especially since the onset of multiple-parent embryos, with the donor egg replacing faulty mitochondria in the mother's egg. Not so in the threads she uncovered: "I'm 32, have Stage 4 uterine cancer, donated three times in my twenties, but docs tell me there's no 'conclusive evidence' that my cancer is a result of the excessive hormones I took. But what's worse is I feel terrible for my good friend, who I convinced to donate along with me. She had all this bleeding after her retrieval. The doctors wanted to send her home, and she refused. Her blood pressure dropped, come to find she was bleeding out. She was in the ER, turns out they nicked an ovarian artery. She had to have numerous blood transfusions. Thank God she lived, but she's infertile now. I feel like I'm to blame." Tasha tore open the box on her knees. Syringes, birth control packs, a To-Do list and calendar illustrated with cute Easter bunny-looking angels.

Was this honestly her best choice to get the money to win back Liam? What assurance did she have that, even if she did get the money legally deposited, the authorities would release him? Three donation cycles would take months; what might happen to Liam in the meantime? He might be tortured, killed, and she'd be putting her health and life in jeopardy, for what? Plastic sheaths slipped as she sifted the box's contents. If there was another, better way, she couldn't think of one. She'd heard the stories of acquaintances who kept profiles on the sugar lifestyle apps, how that was prostitution in everything but name; someone from college had been date-raped by a 'daddy,' forced to have the child and share custody with the rapist. And someone who used to belong in Liam's circle, they'd heard, sold a kidney for a hefty price, but that was black market. No one had heard from him recently, and so assumed him to have been disappeared. Black market money was too suspicious, anyway. She thought of Rafkin—they'd spoken more the last two encounters than they ever had previously. How much could she trust him?

Her MiniSlate vibrated twice in quick succession. One message welcomed her as a new member of the organic supermarket nearby, the other sent to verify her membership at the fitness center, "courtesy of Donor Angels." How long had it been since she'd taken a yoga or barre class? Maybe the adverse effects wouldn't be so bad; maybe she could, for a brief time, eat well and exercise. Stock up, legally, on nutritious real foods, that might be useful to their efforts later, once Liam was back. Rising, she accidentally kicked the box, rattling the bottles of vitamins and supplements at the bottom.

Rafkin didn't appear surprised when the video call opened, her blurting out, "I did it—I'm enrolled. I don't know if I can go through with this, but I think it's too late. I need to hear what you think. If you know of any other options."

The painter's brows needed to be trimmed, the white hairs jutting out like spider's legs even in glitchy hologram. "You signed," he said slowly, "I didn't think you would."

"I didn't, either." She lifted the box for him to see, raised a syringe. "Here—I'm to start right away. Money's already being transferred. I'm to report my injections on the online portal, take fitness classes three times a week. I feel so stupid. I wish there was some other way."

"Don't crucify yourself. There may be, yet, another solution."

"How do I get out of this?"

"You don't. Once they own your body, they own you. But I'd be more worried about time, if I were you."

"You think this is all a waste? That they'll get rid of Liam that quickly?"

"Possibly. There may be something else. Since you left the other day, I've made some inquiries. Both of us would have to work quickly, and if you get enough of the money you need, in perhaps a week or two, you may be able to terminate this donor contract."

"The alternative—you're okay with it?"

"I wouldn't say that. But I'm willing to go along. You might call the offer an extension of our current project." He described a client, politically powerful, who had commissioned the latest series of nudes. This client especially liked her, had anonymously—through the ring Rafkin worked for—asked Rafkin two months ago if the painter thought the girl would be willing to pose for less tasteful portraits. "What he wanted was nothing I wanted to spend my skills on, not to mention exploitative. So I never mentioned it to you, told him no up front. But after your visit the other day I had my contacts put me in touch with him. He is still very interested."

"So he wants fine art porn. Well, okay, who cares? Your style is so impressionistic anyway."

"Let me describe first what he wants. A master is capable of different styles, remember? When I trained, I turned out my share of figures and landscapes. My commissioners know this." Rafkin described then, gruffly, low voiced, what the client wanted. Her dreaded curiosity turned to disgust. No costumes this time, no closed legs, no innocent gazes. So far the client did not request she have a partner, though, and she let go a breath of relief, despite the knot in her gut. *Animal, vegetable, mineral*, was all she could think. One of the arrangements involved her upside-down with a candle protruding from inside her, the lit flame dripping wax.

"So you'd have to be doing these things in front of me, holding poses for a long time, unless you want me to work from photos. And even if we delete those there's the digital trace. There's no telling if a hacker might get ahold of them."

She grimaced, a ripple of dread from head to toe, asked about payment. The client guaranteed that the funds appeared as legal for them both, no government flags.

"But the donor cycle—I can't just not do that. I mean, if I don't take the injections and make the entries, they'll know. They'll know if I don't check into yoga classes or not."

"So make your entries. Go to yoga, buy your organics. Just don't take the hormone shots. We'll have finished the paintings before you are due for the first harvest anyway, and you'll have the money to terminate your contract, plus bail out Liam. And run."

"Outsmart them? You think that's possible?"

"Outsmarting tyrants at their own game is the only strategy we have ever had, my dear," he said. "This may be very good practice, if you and Liam intend to stay alive." They settled on a time, his hologram disintegrated. She poured a vitamin from the bottle and swallowed it.

*

"LIAM FISCHER, IE #407-32-7899, in holding for 50 days before transfer to a Work Zone, to be released only upon bond payment made in full for the amount of $3.3 million U.S. dollars, nonnegotiable." From her MiniSlate a hologram of Liam rotated before her, lip cut and swollen, eyes staring out from blackened sockets. But his cold, dead-on stare told her he hadn't given in and told them anything. No word of where he was being held, or why—of course, for what did citizens need to know except that I.E.s posted a threat to the collective? The good news was whoever he knew in the underground would have seen the posted bond/bail by now, too; someone might reach out to her, and they might double their efforts at gaining his release. The image kept rotating, a full-sized Liam, so that whoever was watching got a clear view of handcuffs and a grey jumpsuit, until she couldn't stand to look any longer and quit the stream.

Her MiniSlate beeped its check-in as she entered the fitness center. She filled her water bottle at the reverse-osmosis tank, did her best to mirror the attendees' faces, upbeat and unperturbed—all was well in the world of those who could afford to come here, maintain regimens of spinning and yoga. Cat, cow, downward dog, plank, and in between she caught herself fantasizing about how this might be her real life. To those around her, the substance of their lives was certainly real. But then the class transitioned into the upright poses, warrior one, warrior two, and a handcuffed Liam resurfaced— hard to pretend that the ugliness outside the controlled and fabricated didn't exist. Her legs trembled, sweat trickled. She tasted salt, focused on the breath. Reverse warrior. Exalted warrior—that was the one she loved best.

In the supermarket she bought a bag of basmati rice, the largest they had, dried fruit, nuts, and pasta, GMO-free. What a feeling to buy anything you wanted, only the best, to barely notice your MiniSlate bleeping its deduction as you exited the doors! She had to remind herself the feeling was false, that for this comfort and luxury she'd signed on as a slave. False liberation, when what the Resistance focused on was a true one. At home she logged into her Donor Angels profile, logged her check-ins at the yoga class and the supermarket, its itemized receipt of all items purchased, and ticked off the dated box beside "Hormonal Dose." Then she arranged half of the food in the cupboard, hid the other half among the Christmas decorations.

*

No photos, they agreed. Not because she had some reputation to protect if a random hacker blasted them across the Internet. But the last thing she needed was facial recognition software to alert the Morality Police. No one posed for free, so where was the money? And, therefore, her taxes? Not to mention the fake ID. They were true believers, those agents; they wouldn't take no for an answer, and she didn't need such complications.

"I'll try to be quick," Rafkin told her apologetically, his droopy face already wearing a look of embarrassment when she disrobed and stood before him, hands folded, ready for the first pose. "Although at my age, I'm hardly the world's speediest painter."

"I'd rather you focus on getting it right," she said. "The last thing I want are any do-overs."

A candle, an antique hairbrush and mirror, a jar of blood. Limbs overhead, no support, the urge to scream worse than ever. The fan's breeze chilled her front, kept going the flame's dance. Wax dripped and stung, cooled and stuck. This body, not hers. Dust shook from the yellow bristles, the hairbrush tarnished almost to black. She used her tricks, found her spot to stare, froze and blinked. Imagined a gun to her head, a blade at her throat. Not difficult. She wished. Until the next pose, candle snuffed out, and she had to hold the oval mirror with one hand while the brush occupied the other. The humiliation a punishment—for what? For her poverty, her vulnerability, his power, this mysterious patron? She could almost hear the stranger laughing. Her cheeks flamed. A bubble rose in her throat. She swallowed hard, mouth dry. Blood dried to brown streaks.

"Enough," Rafkin's voice wavered from somewhere in the shadows. Shakily she arose. Her grasp closed around a cloth, hot and wet. She inhaled a faint odor of citrus.

"The airplanes used to come around and give you those, on international flights," Rafkin said. "Oh, and sushi restaurants, yes, I remember." He nodded, smiling slightly, his tone fond. Sushi was illegal now; such places had all closed.

"Thank you," she mumbled. "Sushi, I could care less. What I could use now is a bath and some hot chocolate."

"You can probably have all of that you want, soon enough. Maybe he'll even give a bonus, this client," Rafkin said, taking back the cloth and handing her the robe. "Myself, all I'd like is some real coffee. I'd say almonds too, but I can't have nuts." His moustache twitched.

*

A week passed, then another. Only thirty-three more days, and Liam would be sentenced, gone. She had posed for five of the six paintings commissioned by Rafkin's client, the old man waking early and continuing to work on the canvases. Small dusty fans oscillated and rattled before the canvases whenever she arrived at nightfall; the sooner they would be dry enough to ship, the sooner she would have her money. One night she brought Rafkin a gift: a pound of whole bean coffee. He tore open the bag and inhaled, smiling.

One evening before yoga, on a night Rafkin decided to work on the paintings alone, she had just updated her Donor Angels profile when a chat avatar popped up—Alicia. "Time for a quick live check-in?" said the text, and before Tasha could respond, the video stream was beeping for her to answer. Might as well get it over with.

A 3-D Alicia, still in lab coat, beamed life-size from the MiniSlate. "So, everything on track, I see? Almost time for your retrieval. How are you feeling?"

"Oh, just fine. I mean, a bit uncomfortable from time to time, and"—Tasha recalled the web forums—"moody. But the yoga helps. Thanks for that fitness pass. I'm heading there right now actually."

"Ah, good. Just a moment. We'll need to arrange to bring you in for the procedure—let's see, three weeks from tomorrow. I have you down for one o'clock. We'll send a car."

The MiniSlate vibrated as the surgery appointment appeared on her profile calendar.

"Just one more thing—if you don't mind setting down that yoga mat, I'm going to do a quick biometric scan from your MiniSlate. Just to quickly measure your vitals. If you'll just set the tablet on a firm surface at least three feet from you—there. Perfect."

"Sure." She dropped the bag, let out a measured exhale. The narrow blue beam landed at her crown and swept downward, then beeped.

"Thank you. Blood pressure very good for this level of hormonal treatment, if a little high. Heart rate, too. Do you find the process of becoming a Donor Angel stressful, Tasha? Any negative thoughts?"

"No, but—it is a big change, that's all. Like I said, I've found the yoga a big help. But I'm about to miss my class."

Alicia nodded—difficult to deduce her expression in glaring hologram, but her lips remained pressed in a small smile as she nodded and signed off.

On the mat Tasha's legs remained watery; no matter how much she concentrated on her breath, her balance felt off. She had to modify her poses almost as soon as she got into them. Once the class transitioned into the more strenuous poses, a pain shot up her hamstring. She got up and limped out, consulted with the fitness desk. "You pulled something," the sports therapist on duty said, and gave her instructions on how to rest and ice the hamstring.

By the following day she could barely walk. She showed up at the warehouse the next night and Rafkin had to help her; finally she slumped onto the tatty armchair beside his easel. "Holding poses is out of the question," he said, shaking his head, frowning. "What do you want to do? Postpone this last painting?"

"I don't see how. We don't have time."

"And Liam's circle? No one has been in touch?"

"No one. Maybe they've picked up a bunch of them, too? I don't know. They're scattered. I have no idea who they are."

"So you are determined to proceed?"

She nodded. "You had better get out your camera. I can manage a pose long enough for you to get some shots. Can you print them out, work from those?"

Rafkin shifted his weight. His grey slacks had tiny holes in the seams. Hand on hip, he shook his head. "No printer, no paper. And the screen is so small I'll have to transfer the photos to the bigger screen, I'm afraid. But we can delete them as soon as possible, I promise."

On the stovetop a pot of water rolled to a boil, and moments later, the singular aroma of coffee consoled her in a way that she'd long forgotten. When she and Liam had first met three years ago, he had impressed her with what he could obtain on the black market: coffee, chocolate, red wine, loose-leaf tea. Liam would wake her up with a cup of coffee in bed every morning, careful to plug towels underneath the doors and windows to hide the scent from the neighbors. In the square of sunlight Rafkin slurped from his mug with one hand, pointed with an index finger as he grasped the paintbrush. "There's your prop," he said. In a murky mason jar were stacked about a dozen eggs. He explained where they were to be applied, and how—some of the raw yolks to be left intact, others to retain their shells. He turned off the fans, apologized that the shoot would be cold and messy.

For the last time she arranged herself, this time on a feather-coated canvas tarp. Rafkin handed her the jar, turned his back. The yolks landed; she recoiled each time. These eggs, with their palest of centers, did they even contain the possibility of bearing chicks? Had they been grown entirely in a lab? Rafkin had likely bought the cheapest he could find. The shells, so thin, crumpled in her hand like tissue paper. Was this what was left of life on earth now: faded remnants of the original blueprints, living things a facsimile of themselves? If they had drifted so far away from the original, dragging all the other creatures along with them, was living still worth the hassle? In ancient times the hopeless drank hemlock; no doubt a pharmaceutical alternative could be given out now if the best one could hope for was to muddle through in this. Two yolks drifted toward one another, a pair of zombie eyes, watery and yellow. Rafkin stooped, snapping shots.

And yet, as the hot spots burned beneath her propped elbows, and her slight breathing shimmied the ova across her top (thank goodness she had never taken those hormonal injections!) she had to admit this was ridiculous. "Am I over-easy or sunny-side-up?" she asked.

"Over-easy." Rafkin paused. "With a little seasoning I'd say eggs benedict." They laughed. He swiped the photos from his MiniSlate to the larger flat screen. "That's a wrap," he said at last. She hopped to her feet, used a towel and bucket of warm water to wash off.

Once she was dressed, Rafkin set down his tablet, offered his arm. She leaned on him until they reached the door. "Get some rest," he said, and patted her shoulder. "You're in good hands, now have faith that our dark lord with a taste for kink, whoever he may be, sends the money, and you can post that bond. Not too long ago I would never have dreamed I would say this, but—sometimes, when the darkness falls across your path like a tree limb, you must use it to climb up. Sometimes that's the only way to reach the light."

*

Days later, waves of estrogen flooding her cells, fogging her mind, she fought to recall events as they had unraveled after the sessions with Rafkin. Helicopters landed on the roof of the building next door. The blades grated her nerves, churned the overwhelming urge to break out of her skin. Think—nothing but time now to do that, if only she could, clearly. What had gone so terribly wrong? Had she been foolish to believe Rafkin had deleted the photos, or that deleting the files would protect them? She shifted and moaned. Her calves ached; impossible to get comfortable with these pangs of pain. The anonymous client had been pleased, that she knew, had her account credited with installments in the sum they had agreed upon. She posted the bail, messaged through her Donor Angel portal that she had decided to cancel the contract, would pay whatever penalty amount was required. Her retrieval date passed; she stayed home, pacing and eating the last of the chocolate, wondering if she would ever see Liam again, or if the money was merely gone.

Twenty-four hours later, the white van pulled up, trailed by another, smaller vehicle. Two white-suited agents opened the center doors, and Liam stumbled into the grass, squinting. She hurried toward him. They embraced. She cradled his hand in hers, had just enough time to register the black and blue marks on his knuckles, the bruises and scrapes, before a familiar voice sounded at her side. "We wondered what happened to you yesterday," Alicia said, stepping forth. The lab coat was gone, replaced with white scrubs. On either side, the white guards who had released Liam now gripped her arms, steered her toward the small vehicle behind the van. She'd planted her feet, asked what was this about, didn't they get her message saying she'd pay the penalty for canceling the contract? "There is no cancellation policy, my dear," Alicia said, following as the men half-carried Tasha over the grass. "Once you sign, the donation is binding. The penalty, in fact, is that you will remain in our facility for the maximum number of retrieval cycles, which is not three, but six. You forfeit any compensation. Not to mention your case will be forwarded onto the Morality Police once your stay with us is terminated. Trying to bribe us out of breaking your contract is, in fact, illegal." The last words she heard before she was shoved in the vehicle, doors locked, Liam's shouts echoing, the agents in their glaring white climbing into the van ahead.

For now she had to forget Rafkin, forget Liam, even. She wasn't allowed visitors. Beyond the bulletproof glass of her isolation cube came the muffled chat of two Eggselent Alternatives! nurses as they put their heads together, discussing e-charts. Several times a day someone entered, took her vitals, gave her a sedative, then the shots. Six retrievals would keep her here for several years, if she lived. Rafkin, she hoped, had been left alone to his warehouse, passing on bundles of lemons from his ailing tree out back to the other girls. By Christmas, Liam would find the food she'd hidden among the decorations, could maybe host an old-fashioned holiday dinner. She rolled over and touched her abdomen, heavy and distended.

ACKNOWLEDGMENTS

I would like to express my gratitude to the following: Vermont College of Fine Arts, where some of these stories began, and my teachers there: Douglas Glover, Xu Xi, Robin Hemley and Domenic Stansberry. Numerous stories here were composed and reimagined at conferences and workshops, under the most generous and wise of teachers: the Sewanee Writers' Conference and Diane Johnson, Bread Loaf Writers' Conference, Margot Livesey and Lan Samantha Chang, the Atlantic Center for the Arts and Victoria Redel, The Banff Centre Writing Studio and Caroline Adderson, and the Key West Literary Seminars and Margaret Atwood. Heartfelt thanks to Escape to Create, Newnan ArtRez, The Rensing Center, Brush Creek Foundation for the Arts, and the Florida Division of Cultural Affairs for the crucial gift of time, space, and fellowship awards. To Sanford J. Greenburger Associates and my agent, Matthew Bialer, and his dauntless championing of my work. To the team at Curbside Splendor Publishing: Victor David Giron, Naomi Huffman, Catherine Eves, and especially editors Josh Bohnsack and Joe Demes, for their sharp eyes and commitment. To Alban Fischer, for another striking and resonant cover. To Kim Britt, John King, Susan Fallows, and Robin Rozanski, for their humor and friendship. To my family, especially Lauren

O'Regan and Sharon Faelten, for their unwavering and enthusiastic support.

And lastly, to Mark Piszczek, my great love and kindred spirit, my house of refuge amidst the storm.

VANESSA BLAKESLEE is the author of *Juventud*, winner of the IPPY 2016 Bronze Medal in Literary Fiction. Her debut collection, *Train Shots*, won the 2014 IPPY Gold Medal in Short Fiction and was long-listed for the 2014 Frank O'Connor International Short Story Award. Her writing has appeared in *The Southern Review*, *Green Mountains Review*, *The Paris Review Daily*, *Kenyon Review Online*, and elsewhere. She lives in Florida.